He Was Jealous! If Only She Could Tell Him the Truth . . .

Pierre dropped his head in his hands. "What happened after the champagne?"

"He and I danced," Willow answered him reluctantly.

"Oh, yes? How?" He lifted his head, staring her intently in the eye.

"How do you think? Standing up facing each other and moving our feet in time to the music."

"I suppose his arms were around you?"

"Of course."

"And yours were around his neck? And your head was on his shoulder?" His words came out in a rush and his eyes were burning hotly into hers. "You enjoyed it, admit it—"

"All right," Willow interrupted. "I did enjoy it. I adored it. It was like dancing on air; dancing in heaven. I could have gone on and on because . . ."

"Yes?"

"Because I imagined I was dancing with—"

KERRY VINE

lives in a seventeenth-century cottage in Hampshire, England. Before she took up writing romances she was an actress. *Alpine Idyll* is Kerry Vine's first Silhouette Romance.

Dear Reader:

I'd like to take this opportunity to thank you for all your support and encouragement of Silhouette Romances.

Many of you write in regularly, telling us what you like best about Silhouette, which authors are your favorites. This is a tremendous help to us as we strive to publish the best contemporary romances possible.

All the romances from Silhouette Books are for you, so enjoy this book and the many stories to come.

Karen Solem
Editor-in-Chief
Silhouette Books

KERRY VINE
Alpine Idyll

Silhouette ❤ *Romance*

Published by Silhouette Books New York

America's Publisher of Contemporary Romance

SILHOUETTE BOOKS, a Division of Simon & Schuster, Inc.
1230 Avenue of the Americas, New York, N.Y. 10020

ISBN: 0-671-57264-4

First Silhouette Books printing December, 1983

10 9 8 7 6 5 4 3 2 1

Map by Ray Lundgren

America's Publisher of Contemporary Romance

Printed in the U.S.A.

BC91

Alpine Idyll

SOUTHERN FRANCE

Places in _italics_ are fictitious.

ALPS

FRANCE

ITALY

RHONE RIVER

PROVENCE

Columbaia

Riviera

Avignon

Ventimille

Nice

Menton

Cannes

Monte Carlo

Monaco

Aix

Marseilles

Toulon

MEDITERRANEAN SEA

Chapter One

"Don't you dare overdo things!" Aunt Ruth had warned as she kissed Willow good-bye at Heathrow Airport. "Just remember that you are going to the south of France to recuperate from pneumonia, not to gad about all hours of the day and night!"

At the time it had seemed an irrelevant warning but now, five hours later, Willow was forced to acknowledge the wisdom of Ruthie's words. The flight and the drive from Nice to Menton on the "wrong" side of the road had exhausted her, and she was longing to reach the village and settle into her accommodations.

Suddenly she spotted the sign she had been looking for. Colombaia. It sounded peaceful—a place where she could rest and recharge her physical and emotional batteries—exactly what she needed after the last hectic six months.

Shifting down into third gear she began to ascend the twisting mountain road leading to the village. The little car she had rented in Nice cruised easily up the steep grade, hugging the sharp bends tightly, and soon the houses with their bright, flower-festooned balconies began to thin out. After a few minutes she passed under the giant viaduct which carried the autoroute into Italy and found herself in another world. A world bounded on one side by a massive rock face, and on the other by a low wall, and a sheer drop into the valley below.

The afternoon sunlight shimmered on the surrounding rocks and bathed the long grasses and the yellow broom lining the valley slopes in a golden glow. Far away lay Menton, first on the left then, as she rounded a bend, on the right: a sprawling arrangement of red roofs and white buildings coming to an abrupt halt in the curve of an incredibly blue sea. The Mediterranean. A very different kettle of fish from the gray-green water lapping the beach at her hometown of Brighton! She took a deep breath of exhilarating mountain air and suddenly felt joyously free. Free from the constraints of home and her father's illness; free from the responsibilities of her new job; free, in fact, to be completely herself, Willow Hale, for the first time in her life.

Hearing the engine strain she shifted into second gear, squeezed 'round a hairpin bend, and drove full tilt into a thick shroud of mist. Switching on the lights, she slowed the car and crawled along, keeping to the center of the narrow road. She had been prepared for a nerve-wracking drive, but had certainly not counted on doing it in a sea fog.

Without warning a large stationary object loomed up a few meters ahead and she braked sharply. A lorry. What a place to park! Cautiously she eased the car forward. There was just enough room to slip between it and the rock face and, taking her courage in both hands, she was about to accelerate through the gap when a pair of yellow headlights swept around the corner and another car pulled up on the far side of the lorry.

She sat back and waited but the other driver, instead of attempting to reverse, merely tooted the horn gently, as much as to say, well get on with it then! Willow bit her lip nervously; the fog, pressing in from all sides, made it impossible to see anything. She could not risk reversing. After a few minutes a solid, denim-clad arm emerged from the lorry window and made unmistakable backing gestures in her direction. Still she waited. After all, the car was probably driven by a local who would find it much easier to back in the restricted space than she would. The horn blared again, this time loudly, impatiently.

Willow frowned. However great the other driver's hurry there was no call for a display of bad manners. Nevertheless he obviously did not intend to make the first move, added to which it was a case of two against one. Anyway there seemed nothing for it but to give in, and grudgingly putting the car into reverse gear she jerked gingerly backwards. Calculating that she had about five meters visibility she slowly began to nudge the car into its original position behind the lorry. It was like playing a hazardous version of blind man's buff. She kept stopping and craning her neck out of the window to see where she was going. Beads of perspiration began to break out on her upper lip. This is absurd, she told herself severely, you have been driving in all weather conditions for over two years, why panic now?

Suddenly the mist, harried by a playful breeze, lifted briefly and in the thirty seconds that followed she had an all too clear view of her situation. Somehow she had managed to reverse the car into a diagonal position so that it stood with its rear wheels within inches of the low, crumbling parapet and the abyss beyond. A foot farther and. . . . Trembling with shock she yanked on the brake, switched off the engine and sat clutching the steering wheel in an agony of fear.

After what seemed like an aeon but could only have been minutes, a car door slammed and a tall, broad-shouldered figure walked toward her out of the mist and, stooping down, looked in the open window. Her first impression was of a lean, tanned face and eyes so clear and blue that she had an instant vision of the Mediterranean. Only then did she notice the pale scar slashed across his left cheekbone like a river running between golden, sandy banks. After that she became aware of his derisive expression and her stomach muscles contracted nervously.

"Je regrette, Monsieur, que je me trouve dans

une situation difficile," she stammered awkwardly. A difficult situation indeed. More like an impossible one! It was six years since she had passed French O Level, even so she should have been able to manage a less crass statement of her position.

The faintest gleam of humor flickered in the blue eyes. "Girls who are afraid of heights should not be in charge of dangerous machines on precipitous mountain roads," he said, in perfect English.

Willow's chin shot up defensively. "You obviously saw I was in difficulties. Why didn't you go back yourself? I thought Frenchmen were supposed to be so gallant!"

"Really?" He lifted an amused eyebrow. "Then I cannot destroy an illusion. Allow me to demonstrate that the age of chivalry is not dead." And without waiting for an answer he opened the car door, pushed both hands under her body and shifted her unceremoniously over into the passenger seat. He then settled himself behind the wheel and proceeded slowly, but expertly, to maneuver the car into a safe position at the side of the road.

"Voilà!" he said, switching off the engine. "You think you can manage it yourself next time?"

His face was serious, but his voice held a teasing note. He was definitely laughing at her. She realised that he was older than she had first thought, thirty-five perhaps. His thick dark hair was lightly salted with gray, and two lines traversed his face vertically from his nose to his square jaw. His mouth, although amiable at the moment, had a folded, bitter look and there was that ugly scar. . . . Not a person to tangle with, Willow decided.

Suddenly he laughed: a deep, rich sound which rang out across the valley. "Don't look so outraged. I am not about to eat you!"

Willow forced herself to breathe deeply. She was not frightened, but her heart was beating with a strange uneven action, as if doing an old-fashioned fox trot. Slow, slow, quick, quick, slow. "I think," she said firmly, "that you have made your point. Now I would like to proceed with my journey."

"Of course." But it was said absently and he made no attempt to move. Instead he let his eyes rove impersonally over her face and body as if she were an exhibit at a museum: a rare artifact or piece of fine porcelain. She felt herself growing uncomfortably warm under this intimate examination but continued to stare back with an air of calm expectancy she was far from feeling. "Well, can I go now?" she said at last.

He did not reply and she was about to order him to move when he leaned forward, took her face between his hands and kissed her lightly but lingeringly on the lips. Seconds later he was out of the car and looking in the window again.

"After all," he said, "you did not say thank you did you?" And straightening up he strode away and was soon swallowed by the mist.

Before she had time to recover a silver Ferrari zoomed past and the roar of its engine became fainter and fainter as it dropped down the mountain until she could no longer hear it. Only then did she feel composed enough to climb back into the driving seat. Glancing in the mirror she was surprised to see her flaming cheeks and the dazed expression in her eyes. "Cool it Willow," she said aloud.

Ten minutes later she was driving thankfully up the narrow road leading into Colombaia, and reaching the main *place*—or square—she parked the car under a tree and got out. Aunt Ruth had instructed her to collect the key from Madame Leduc at the Hotel Clemenceau.

Clutching a useless guide book to her chest like a talisman, she passed hopefully under dripping archways and climbed endless steps in dank twisting alleys searching for the elusive hotel. But the whole village seemed deserted, and the drifting vapor never lifted long enough to give her a complete picture of the scene. Occasionally disembodied voices floated through half-open windows, and once a cat shot past intent on urgent business of its own, but otherwise there was no sign of life.

She was about to knock on a door and ask for directions when she spotted the name Clemenceau in faded red letters above a doorway and, greatly relieved, went inside. It appeared to be more of a restaurant than a hotel and a tubby little man with a shining face and slick black hair was busily wiping down the tables. He stopped as soon as he saw her.

Willow smiled. "Monsieur Leduc?"

"At your service, Mademoiselle. What can I do for you?" He spoke guttural French and, moving to the wall, switched on the lights to get a better look at his visitor.

Willow, uneasily aware of the Frenchman's admiring gaze, spoke more abruptly than she intended. *"Parlez vous anglais, Monsieur?"*

"Mais oui, Mademoiselle, I speak a little English. How can I help you? You would like a room perhaps?"

"No thank you."

"No? What a pity."

His face assumed an expression of such comical sadness that Willow laughed aloud. "I am sure you are not short of guests at this time of year," she said.

He made a little bow. "We always have room for beautiful girls."

It was time to come to the point. "I think I am supposed to collect the key to Nine Rue des Fleurs from you. I wrote to you last week."

Monsieur Leduc smacked his glistening forehead with the flat of his hand as if to enliven his brains. "Of course, of course! What am I thinking of? My wife Anna knows all about it. But you must be tired, Mademoiselle. It is not good for visitors to drive to Colombaia for the first time through *la brume.* The mist, you understand."

She nodded. "It was terrible."

"I am so sorry but you are safe now and soon that road will be an old friend."

She smiled wanly. "I hope you're right. At this moment I need reviving with a cup of strong coffee."

"Coffee, but certainly!"

Monsieur Leduc sprang into action and Willow

sat down to rest at a table by the window. When he returned she was gazing out at the blank world beyond the hotel.

"You are disappointed," he said, putting down the cup. "Nothing to see, eh? It is the fault of the mist. Tomorrow you will see everything I promise. Maybe even before tomorrow."

"Good." She sipped the black coffee gratefully. "Somehow I didn't expect the village to be like this—buried in layers of cotton-wool."

"Cotton-wool?"

"*L'ouate,*" she said, groping through memories of French lessons long past for the right word to enlighten him.

"*L'ouate,* ah yes." He nodded wisely several times but she could see that he still did not understand.

"You do not speak French, Mademoiselle?"

She shook her head. "Very little. I manage better in Italian."

"Italian eh?" His round face lit up with pleasure. "That is good. My wife Anna, she is Italian. Many people in Colombaia are Italian. We are very close to the border here."

"I know. I read all about it before I left England. This whole area has only been part of France since about 1880. My mother was Italian. She taught me to speak it when I was little."

"An Italian Mama, *c'est bien.*" Monsieur Leduc chuckled approvingly and rocked backwards and forwards on his heels. "She would like Colombaia, this Italian lady. Why is she not with you?"

His guest's lovely green eyes clouded over and

she made a pretense of stirring her coffee. "My mother died years ago."

"That is very sad." He allowed a moment of respectful sympathy to elapse and then swiped at a dozy fly on the windowpane with his cloth. "These wretched insects—God sends them to plague me!" Turning 'round he broke into a torrent of French which Willow managed to translate freely as, "Anna, come quickly. The English mademoiselle is here. She wants the key to Number Nine. It is on the table in the office next to Grandfather's teeth."

Minutes later a small shriveled woman appeared in the doorway and advanced toward them. Her shrewd brown eyes summed up Willow's exhausted state immediately.

"The poor little one. She is tired," she said to her husband.

He nodded. "It is best to go now." He turned to Willow. "My wife will help carry your luggage to the house. It is necessary to leave your car in the square. You will please come here if there is anything you need."

She thanked him and left the hotel with Madame Leduc. At first they walked in constrained silence, then she plucked up courage to address her companion in her native tongue.

"You are Italian, Signora?"

The woman flashed her a look of surprise. "The Signorina speaks Italian?"

"A little. My mother taught me."

They collected the luggage from the car and recrossed the square, their footsteps ringing out on the wet stones. Somewhere above their heads the church clock chimed two o'clock on a clear, flat note.

"How long will the mist last?" asked Willow.

Anna shrugged. "Who knows? A few hours—a few days. It has been bad this year."

She led the way down a flight of long cobbled steps descending between the high walls of old houses. At the bottom they turned left and tramped through a gloomy tunnel under two more houses, finally emerging into yet another alley. Madame Leduc stopped in front of a brown door, fished the key out of her apron pocket and turned it in the lock.

"Enter, Signorina," she said, and Willow stepped into a small hall with a black-and-white tiled floor and rough plastered walls. Through an archway she caught a glimpse of a rustic kitchen with a large table, and geraniums on the window ledge. Anna, who was already halfway up the spiral stairs, called over her shoulder, "Come Signorina. I will put the suitcase in the bedroom." Obediently, Willow followed her up to the next floor.

The dim light filtering through the closed shutters revealed a room furnished with an antique wardrobe, a dressing table with an old gilt mirror and a carved chair. A large bed with a carved headboard dominated most of the space and she longed to crawl under the covers and go to sleep. The house seemed to be brooding, waiting perhaps for something or someone; she had the strangest feeling of familiarity, as if she had known it all her life.

Anna pointed at a door on the tiny landing.

"The bathroom," she said, but before Willow had time to investigate she said, "This way Signorina," and again Willow followed the stocky, black-clad legs up another short flight of stairs and found herself on the top floor, in a charming sittingroom. Here too the shutters of the long windows were closed, but the half-light enabled her to take in the coarsely woven rugs, and sofa and chairs strewn with comfortable cushions. A terracotta pot of marigolds glowed in the center of the stone fireplace.

"It's all lovely," she breathed contentedly.

Anna just smiled and, like a magician approaching the climax of his act, opened the windows and flung away the shutters revealing a delightful balcony, gay with tubs of mixed flowers spilling casually over the edge of their containers. As Willow stepped outside a sudden breeze ruffled her hair and the mist slowly lifted and wafted away. Anna's magic was complete. Around them the mountains stood proudly; their terraced flanks punctuated with dark, needle cypresses; their sharp, rocky peaks etched, like jagged sentinels, against the blue sky. Far below, the road along which she had driven snaked down the mountainside in a series of tight bends until it plunged out of sight. Several kilometers away the sea sparkled in the sunlight. To her intense delight she realized that the little house, perched on the outer rim of the village, enjoyed an uninterrupted view of the mountains and the green, fertile valley. She opened her arms wide, her young face alight with pleasure. *"Bellissima!"*

Anna nodded. She had, of course, timed the

whole thing perfectly, albeit with a little help from nature, but it was good to hear the beautiful view praised by the pretty English girl. "Si Signorina. But now you must rest a little. You can always find me at the hotel," she said, stumping off down the stairs.

Dreamily Willow allowed her gaze to travel from the cultivated valley up the tree-sprinkled hillsides to the azure sky above and, for no apparent reason, she thought of the blue-eyed stranger who had kissed her only an hour before. It had been an outrageous thing to do and her cheeks burned at the memory. She was not likely to run into him again of course, but if she did she would make it clear that she did not . . . she would certainly tell him that . . . give him to understand that such behaviour. . . . The age of chivalry indeed! Steve would have been furious. Steve. How strange, she had not thought of him once since she boarded the plane. Guiltily, she turned her back on the glorious view and went down the spiral stairs to the bedroom. Anna was right. She needed to rest.

Chapter Two

The room was cool and restful and, removing her sandals, she lay down on the bed. Then, on impulse, she got up, unlocked her suitcase, and taking out a leather-framed photograph stood it on the bedside table. It was a good photograph, one she had taken herself. The red tractor looked both powerful and homely set against the sloping brown furrows of Ten-Acre Field, and Steven—fair-haired, ruddy-complexioned Steve—seemed to epitomize the healthy young farmer. She got back onto the bed, closed her eyes and shut out the laughing face.

It was an uncomfortable feeling being engaged, and yet not being engaged. Unsettling. If only he would agree to make it official and get on with the whole thing. His reasons for delaying were beginning to sound rather hollow: he could not disturb his mother who was getting over an operation; the farm was not yet profitable enough to support his parents and a family of his own; he was certain things would be better next year. She must be patient. In vain she argued that her recent promotion meant she could contribute substantially to their finances; there was no need to be a drag on the farm income. Steven had merely looked at her with astonishment.

"Do you think I would allow my wife to work?"

She had been startled. The idea that marriage would put an end to her career had never entered her head. "But I like my work," she protested.

He had smiled patronizingly. "Of course my love, but you must surely see that it wouldn't be at all suitable for you to be the manageress of a flower shop after we are married."

"But it is only the beginning," she said. "One day I will have a chain of shops—my own shops."

He had declined to discuss it further and, not for the first time, Willow found herself suppressing feelings of deep resentment. Somehow she must get him to take her seriously, acknowledge her as a person, with her own hopes and dreams. But it was going to be difficult.

It had been the proudest day of her life when the Managing Director of Florifair had dropped into the Hove branch and offered her the post. "Mrs. Daly is leaving the Brighton shop," he said, "I would like you to take the job on. After all you have coped with things here often enough in Mr. Troy's absence. You have a very good business head, Miss Hale. I am confident you can make a go of it."

Three weeks later Willow walked into the Brighton branch as the new manageress in charge of a staff of five. It meant greater responsibility than she had ever known, and an enormous increase in her work load, but she was determined to justify the company's faith in her ability.

Apart from Steve's sour reaction, the future augured well, but within a month her father's ill-health plunged them into anxiety and insecurity. For twenty-five years Tom Hale had worked as farm manager for Ben Holder, Steven's father, but when he began to have severe chest pains Mr. Holder insisted on a proper medical checkup. After a series of tests Tom was told that he had a heart condition and must give up his strenuous occupation. Ben Holder was a fair man, but he had a farm to run and needed their house for a new manager. He gave them plenty of time to find somewhere to live, but Tom had no capital to buy a house, and the area was chronically short of rented accommodation.

Finally, Aunt Ruth generously offered to share her bungalow with them. They accepted with gratitude but the strain of coping with the move and the responsibilities of her new position culminated in a bout of neglected flu followed by pneumonia landing Willow in hospital for three weeks. She recovered quickly, but throughout the winter she remained tired and listless and had to force herself to keep up with her heavy schedule. Finally Ruthie stepped in and organized the holiday in Colombaia through a friendly client who came to her hairdressing shop in Peacehaven.

Steven thought the idea was crazy. "It's ridiculous," he said. "You've never been out of England before. You won't know what to do."

It was true. By the age of twenty-two most of her friends had been abroad several times, but Willow's holidays were spent helping out on the farm. They were always shorthanded and she enjoyed the exercise and the open-air life. Anyway she liked being near Steve. Or used to like it. Lately she was not so sure. . . .

She awoke completely refreshed. A glance at her watch revealed that she had been asleep for a couple of hours, and jumping out of bed she opened the shutters and leaned out of the window. Below, in the small overgrown garden, a few dirty white chickens scratched and pecked the ground while a gray cat, curled up on the branch of a young walnut tree, watched them through sleepy, half-closed eyes.

Quickly pulling a periwinkle-blue shirt and wraparound skirt out of her case, she dressed, thrust her feet into sandals and ran down the stairs. A cursory look around the kitchen exposed a total lack of essential foodstuffs. Taking a basket from a slate shelf in the larder she set off in the direction of the main square hoping to find a grocery shop.

The dark alleys which had seemed so forbidding on her arrival were now full of sharp shadows and bright, patchy sunlight. She walked swiftly up the shining cobbled steps, her eyes delighting in the bells of purple campanula overhanging the thick, rough archways and cascading down the flaky stone walls of the old houses.

The shop, squashed between the church and the post office, had *Épicerie* written above the door, and climbing the steps she pushed through the plastic ribbon curtain which served as a doorway. Fortunately there were no other customers and she soon had the few things she needed in her basket.

The afternoon was sunny and the air soft and warm. Willow sauntered across the square, perched herself on the low wall under the trees and gazed dreamily across the valley. Hugging her knees in anticipation she resolved to set out on a voyage of discovery in the morning come rain or shine, and having reached this decision turned her back on the scenery and began to study the populace of Colombaia.

A few men in shirt sleeves were sitting at tables outside the *Bar Et Tabac,* and on the far side of the square a harassed coach driver was herding reluctant tourists into his bus so that he could drive them back to Menton. As she gazed idly around she noticed an old man with a white beard and a shock of white hair emerge from the *Épicerie* carrying a walking stick in one hand and a bag overflowing with groceries in the other. Suddenly he stumbled, and in trying to save himself dropped the bag which promptly split, spilling its contents over the cobbles. Stooping down he began laboriously to reassemble them, but as no one took the slightest notice of his predicament Willow felt compelled to go over and help. Fortunately nothing seemed to have suffered except the tomatoes which were squashed and irretrievable.

He produced a string bag from the inside pocket of his coat and they filled it with his goods. "I knew it was not safe," he said sadly, in French. "I should not have trusted it. You are very kind Mademoiselle."

"Ça ne fait rien Monsieur,"—It is nothing—she replied, wondering how she would manage if the conversation took another turn.

His pale blue eyes twinkled. "You are English I think."

Her face fell. "Oh dear. I suppose my accent gave me away."

"We are not very good at speaking other languages. It's time we mended our ways."

Again the twinkle. "Time you . . . pulled your socks up?"

She laughed. "Anyway you speak good English! Yes, high time we pulled up our socks."

He put out a thin, veined hand and lightly touched her arm. "A loving heart is the most important quality a human being can possess. You need feel no shame, Mademoiselle." And with a courteous little bow he turned and began to walk away. She watched him go, but something about the way he moved and the weary sag of his shoulders made her run after him. "Put some of your things in my basket," she said. "I can easily go back via your house."

His eyes widened with astonishment. "Then you are not human after all. You are an angel."

She grinned. "Now you are teasing."

He smiled. "Perhaps I am. If you will take

this . . ." He handed her a packet of rice. "It will lighten my load and give me the pleasure of your company for a little longer."

"Fine," she agreed, "but in that case I will carry your bag and you will take my basket."

He shook his head in mock disapproval. "How bossy you young women are today. I suppose you will not be satisfied until I do as you say."

She nodded emphatically. "Right."

They left the square and began to climb to the highest level of the village. The old man walked very slowly, often pausing to rest.

"You are on holiday, Mademoiselle?"

"Yes." She looked back at the square. The bus had gone but the men were still sitting under the trees as they must have done for generations. "You know," she said, "Colombaia is not at all what I expected."

"Is that so? And what, I wonder, did you expect?"

Willow shrugged. "I don't quite know. A French version of an English village I think. It is both uglier and more beautiful than I had imagined—if that makes sense."

"Perfectly. You had not imagined dank, gaping cellars, misty echoing passages and legions of emaciated cats."

She frowned. "It is more than that. I had no idea the village would look—and feel—like ancient fortifications. I keep expecting them to pull up the drawbridge and man the battlements."

But he did not laugh. "We have done that too often," he said. "You will find all the old gun emplacements are still standing. Colombaia was an embattled fortress during the war and bears scars to prove it."

After walking for ten minutes they stepped out of the alley into the sunlight at the top of the village. Behind them, dominated by a huge wooden cross, rose the grassy slopes of the mountain in whose protective bosom Colombaia so comfortably nestled.

The old Frenchman stopped in front of a weather-beaten door. "You will allow me to offer you a glass of wine?"

She hesitated. He did not look well enough to bother with a guest. His face was too pale and his hands fumbled weakly with the latch.

"I think perhaps . . ." she began.

His eager expression faded. "Of course. I must not take up more of your time."

"Oh no, it's not that!" she protested. "I would love one. Thank you."

He unlocked the door and stood back for her to enter. "I live in a very humble way," he apologized. "Please do not expect the Ritz."

It may not have been the Ritz, but the room she entered had a charm of its own. It was large and square, with a low ceiling and rough, white walls. A pair of sagging basket chairs stood in front of the range, a long dresser covered with blue china stood against one wall, and a scrubbed table occupied pride of place in the center of the room. The wood floor was unpolished, and bunches of herbs, suspended from the ceiling, filled the air with a subtle aroma as they wafted back and forth in the breeze from the open window.

Willow was reminded of the farmhouse kitchen

she had grown up in and would never see again. "This is a lovely room," she said wistfully.

The old man watched the eager young face drinking in the simple beauty of his home, then he nodded as if satisfied. "Sit down, Mademoiselle," he said. "I will pour us a glass of wine. I think you will find it pleasing. It has a delicate, but lively quality which—you will not mind my saying so— reminds me of you."

She smiled at the compliment and sat down in a chair in front of the fire. There was so much to look at: books and paintings as well as innumerable interesting objects, all lying carelessly on shelves, or on the floor as if the old man frequently picked them up for pleasure and put them down at random. The room had an infectious atmosphere of peace and serenity and Willow gave a long sigh of contentment.

Her host handed her a glass of amber-colored wine and sat down.

"You will not mind if I make a little drawing of you while we talk?"

"No one has ever drawn me before," she said.

He looked surprised. "Is that possible? I thought England was full of discerning artists." Reaching over to a shelf he pulled out a sketch pad, a wooden board and a pencil, and settled them comfortably on his knees. "I think I should tell you my name. It is Anselm. Anselm Castille."

"Mine is Willow Hale."

"Willow." His hand began to move lightly and quickly across the paper. "It is the name of a tree I think. A slender tree which likes to spend its life weeping by water."

She laughed. "Fortunately it has a large family. There are other, happier willows as well as the weeping one."

"I am glad." His eyes darted back and forth from his work to her face. "Where are you staying?"

"In the Rue des Fleurs. Number Nine."

He paused for a moment, an amused expression flitting across his face. "Do you like it there?"

"Oh yes," she replied enthusiastically. "From my balcony I can see right across the valley to the sea. I wonder the owner can bear to let it to strangers."

"A house is only a house," Anselm said gently. "It is people who matter."

"That is just what I mean. Whoever owns that house loves it. It is full of love."

She gave a small, self-deprecating laugh. "You must think I am dotty!"

"Dotty? You are not dotty but you are a very sensitive girl. Now will you please stop waving your pretty hands and let me continue with my sketch!"

An hour later, during which she seemed to have told him the story of her life, he put the completed drawing on the table and stood up. "My old bones do not like to sit still for long." He beckoned her to come and look. "You think it is like you? Have I done you justice? No, I fear I have not."

Willow looked over his shoulder. A stranger stared back at her. A stranger, yet a face she saw in the mirror every day. Was her neck really so

long; were her eyes so large? She experienced a
feeling of incredulity and delight. "Do I really
look like that?"

He smiled wryly. "Unfortunately not. You are
far more interesting."

"I don't suppose. . . ." She hesitated. After
all, the sketch could not mean anything to Anselm, but it would be an original present to take
back to Steven. ". . . I mean would you let me
have it? I would pay for it of course."

He shook his head. "I will not take money from
you but I will make you a gift of it if—it is hardly
fair to ask but you are entitled to refuse—if you
will indulge the whim of an old man and sit for
your portrait."

"My portrait?" She was astounded.

He nodded. "Yes. I am preparing for an exhibition in Paris at the end of the year and you are the
perfect subject."

Something in her expression—sheer amazement perhaps—made him think she was about to
refuse and he turned disconsolately away. "I
know it is a lot to ask. Too much. Too much."

He looked so distressed that she knew she
would have to agree, if only to see him smile
again. Her plans for exploring the countryside
would just have to be fitted 'round the portrait
sessions.

"Of course I will sit for you," she said. "It will
be very exciting. I will begin tomorrow morning if
you like."

His tired face lit up, and taking her hand he
brought it gently to his lips in a charming gesture
of thanks. "After my exhibition," he said, "the

whole of Paris will be, not only at your fingertips, but at your feet." And on this extravagant but altogether delightful note he led her to the door and ushered her into the sunlight.

The next day dawned brightly with no sign of mist. Willow selected a green sun dress from the wardrobe and clasped a string of beads around her throat. After a delicious breakfast of warm croissants, peach jam and coffee, she borrowed a straw sun hat from a hook behind the bedroom door and left the house. It was still early but mouth-watering smells of cooking drifted out of open windows into the streets, and children's piping voices filled the air. Everyone seemed friendly; even the scrawny cats, instead of fleeing as she approached, stayed washing themselves contentedly in the sun. Old women smiled and nodded as she walked by, and swarthy young men in faded jeans fixed her with bold, admiring eyes.

Anna Leduc was standing outside the hotel gossiping with a neighbor. *"Buon giorno Signorina,"* she called.

Willow waved happily. "Good morning, Signora." Already she felt part of the village life, and she was going to make the best of it—even if it was only for a fortnight.

Stepping out of the dark passage onto the open pathway she made directly for Anselm's house. There was no bell but she lifted the knocker and rapped on the door. It opened immediately, but the man standing before her was not Anselm; it was the man she had encountered on the mountain road, the man who had kissed her with such outrageous effrontery. And his expression, far from being pleased, was downright hostile. For a long moment he stared at her with the coldest, bluest eyes she had ever seen. Then he stood aside.

"You'd better come in," he said grudgingly.

Chapter Three

The first thing she saw was the sketch of herself propped against an earthenware jug on the table, but there was no sign of the old man. The familiar, gentle spirit was absent and the room felt chilly in spite of the heat outside.

Hearing the door close she turned. "Where is Anselm? I have an appointment with him."

The Frenchman, seeming in no hurry to reply, strolled over to the window and stood looking out, his back towards her: a broad back tapering to narrow hips above long, restless legs. In his black clothes he looked too large, too powerful to be confined in the low-ceilinged room, and she was uncomfortably reminded of a captive panther waiting to spring to freedom.

"Unfortunately my father was taken ill last night," he said at last.

Willow caught her breath in alarm. "Anselm ill? Is it serious?" Then the full significance of his statement dawned. "Your father? You mean you are . . .?"

He glanced 'round at her flushed, anxious face with its enormous green eyes, but his expression did not soften.

"Yes, I am Pierre Castille."

She made a move towards the door which led to the inner part of the house. "Where is he? What happened? Can I see . . .?"

Brusquely, he cut her short. "He had a fall and suffered slight shock and bruising. He managed to telephone me and of course I came immediately. He is now at my house in Menton. Already he is feeling much better."

She sighed with relief. "Poor Anselm. He did not look at all well yesterday."

Pierre shrugged. "He should not be living alone up here. I've tried to persuade him to leave for years but he's obstinate. Now he must see reason. I'll have all his stuff moved tomorrow and then I'll close this house."

"Against his will?" She could hardly believe her ears. How could anyone be so unfeeling?

"I've told you," he said patiently, "he is very stubborn. He must show some consideration for others. He will be quite happy in my house, and he'll be well looked after. It's the only thing to do."

"But he loves this house," she pleaded. "He belongs here. His whole life is bound up with this village. You can't just pick him up and dump him somewhere else because it happens to suit you! Old people have their rights too you know."

"Even if they die upholding them?"

"Even then."

He stared coldly at her. "There's no need to lecture me about my father, Mademoiselle; I think I understand him better than you although . . ." He glanced at the sketch on the table. "You seem to have made a strong impression in a short time. It is quite a coup to be asked to sit for your portrait by one of the most accomplished artists in France on so slight an acquaintance."

She frowned. "Quite a coup? I don't understand."

"All right. Let's call it a feather in your cap. You see I'm quite good at your English idioms."

Slow anger began to build up inside Willow. "Are you suggesting that I somehow enticed your father into asking me to sit for my portrait?"

"I am merely saying that when people see my father's painting they will want to know who you are. You will be famous. Other artists will want to paint you. The whole world will be interested in Anselm Castille's new model."

"I see." She took a deep breath to steady her voice. "Well it may interest you to know that I never heard of Anselm Castille until yesterday, and if that makes me a fool then so be it! I agreed to sit for your father because it seemed terribly important to him. He is a kind man and I wanted to please him." The hard line of Pierre's mouth did not alter and she turned away in frustration.

"Never mind. I wouldn't expect you to understand."

He raised a sardonic eyebrow. "Oh, but I assure you I do. It was very philanthropic of you Mademoiselle—most generous." He walked over to the table and picked up the sketch. "This is good. He has caught you very well. The cheekbones, the eyes . . ." He put it down and smiled, almost amiably. "It's charming. I imagine you would like to own it. My father too is generous. I expect he offered to give it to you."

"Yes," she said shortly, still smarting from his snide insinuations.

A gleam of triumph appeared in the blue eyes. "You of course have no idea of its value—say one thousand pounds?"

Willow gasped. "A thousand pounds? I don't believe you."

He moved across to the recessed shelves by the window and extracted a large book with a glossy cover. "This is one of a dozen or more books about my father's work. Perhaps you would like to see it?"

Dumbly she shook her head. A thousand pounds! In her ignorance she had virtually asked the old man for a gift worth a thousand pounds. No wonder he had not handed it over immediately! His son could be excused for regarding her as a fortune-hunting adventuress. How could she begin to explain? She raised her shoulders in a little gesture of apology. "I didn't understand. Please believe me."

"Of course," he said, but she could see he was still unconvinced and tears of mortification rushed to her eyes. Before they could overflow and humiliate her further she turned and groped blindly for the door, overcome with a desperate need to get away from Pierre Castille and his nasty, suspicious mind. But as she reached for the latch he made a lightning move across the room, stretched out a long arm and leaned heavily against the door.

"Not so fast. I have a message for you."

He was standing so close that her spine began to tingle, sending alarming, claustrophobic signals to her brain. Desperately she fought off the urge to panic, to lash out, to pull frantically at the door. Instead, she forced herself to stand still and speak calmly. "What message?"

"Ah, so you are interested?"

He was playing cat-and-mouse with her now and she knew it. She stared at the wooden door barring the way to freedom, her mind racing. What did he want? Why was he taunting her? She could feel his warm breath on the nape of her neck. Her knees suddenly felt weak and she put out a hand to steady herself against the wall.

"The message is from my father," he said. "As I said before he is extremely stubborn. He will only stay in my house if he can paint the portrait there. However he thinks it is not fair to ask you as the journey will take up too much of your time. So you see we are all in your hands." He uttered a low laugh. "What price philanthropy now?"

Stung by his mocking tone she spun round to face him, her eyes flashing ominously. "First you accuse me of currying favour with your father out of self-interest, then you expect me to give up a

large slice of my holiday so that you can look after
him with as little trouble to yourself as possible!
Just what do you take me for?"

He smiled grimly. *"Chérie,* I have not taken
you at all yet. When I want you I'll let you know."

Willow heard the crack of her hand against his
cheek before she realized what she had done. It
was all over in a second. He did not attempt to
retaliate, but towered silently over her as if
carved out of stone. Only his icy, glittering eyes,
and a small vein throbbing near his temple gave
any indication of his feelings. She watched, fascinated, as a red weal spread across his scarred
cheek.

"I . . . I . . ." she began, but could not continue. She had been about to apologize, but in the
split second it took to form the words realized
that she had actually enjoyed slapping his face,
that given half a chance she would slap it
again. Since the moment they met his attitude
had become increasingly arrogant and insulting.
The only thing she felt badly about was the
scar.

"Next time," he said quietly, "I will turn the
other cheek."

Caught out in her thoughts she blushed scarlet.

Pierre's arm dropped away from the door and
he stepped back into the room. "Villa Martine,"
he said casually. "In the Garavan district. Anyone will direct you. Shall we say eleven tomorrow
morning?" Moving away he began to flip over the
pages of the art book lying on the table.

"I haven't said I'll come," Willow reminded
him.

"No, but you will." He did not bother to look up.

Halfway down the alley she broke into a furious run. The insufferable pig! Nothing would induce her to go to his house in the morning. She would rather catch the next plane home!

Monsieur Leduc called out as she rushed headlong through the square but she pretended not to hear. Thrusting the key into the lock of Number Nine she turned it and almost fell into the hall. The telephone was ringing. She lifted the receiver.

"Yes?"

The line crackled and buzzed.

"Yes?" she repeated. "Hello?"

"Willow?" The voice was faint but unmistakable.

"Steve!" Her cry of pleasure immediately turned to one of alarm. "Why are you ringing? Is anything wrong? Is it Dad?"

"No, everyone is fine. I just thought . . ."

Crackle. Crackle.

"Steve are you there?"

". . . to see how you are."

Crackle. Silence. Then music, the dim strains of an old ballad. *"Je t'aime, je t'aime,"*—I love you, I love you,—murmured the singer.

"Who is playing that music?"

"I don't know. We must have a crossed line. Do you miss me Steve?"

"What?"

"Do—you—miss—me?"

"Oh. Yes, of course. Bill's away sick. We are very shorthanded."

"That's too bad." It was a good thing he could not see her expression. The music again: *"Je t'aime, je t'aime . . ."*

"Willow? Are you still there? You sound funny."

Why was she always hoping he would change— be warmer, more loving? She brushed her wet cheek with the back of her hand. "I've got a bit of a cold."

"That's rotten luck. Well . . . this is costing a fortune. Better get back to the treadmill I suppose. All work and no play. It's all right for some!"

"Yes. Lucky me. Thanks for ringing. Sorry I am not there to fill in for Bill."

"Never mind. We'll manage. Take care."

"Will do. 'Bye." She replaced the receiver, cutting off the mournful refrain.

Just why had he bothered to ring? Was it to tell her that they were shorthanded on the farm and make her feel guilty? Or because he loved her and needed to hear her voice? It would be comforting to think it was the latter, but in her heart she knew it was not. Steve had phoned to assert his proprietorial rights! She supposed she ought to be flattered.

On a sudden impulse she bent down, took hold of the telephone cord and yanked it out of the wall. For two weeks at least no one, absolutely no one was going to interfere with her freedom. Especially not Pierre Castille!

Throwing wide the shutters the next morning she leaned out of the window and filled her lungs with the sweet air. The mist was clearing from the valley and the sky above the mountains was marvelously blue. It was the perfect day to explore the hills—but for the promise she had given Anselm. She recalled a snatch of poetry she had learned at school.

> The woods are distant dark and deep
> But I have promises to keep,
> And miles to go before I sleep.

Yesterday she had no intention of keeping her word, but this morning she knew she could not let the old man down. It would cost her nothing but time and, if she met Pierre again, a little pride. Anyway he had made his contempt for her so plain that he would probably take care to stay well out of her way.

Driving down the mountain in the crystal clear light was a great deal easier than driving up in a thick fog and the little car swung 'round the bends.

Driving through the villa gates she parked the car under a palm tree and got out, noting with relief that the silver Ferrari was nowhere in sight. She had realized that Pierre was not a poor man but Villa Martine took her breath away. It was long and elegantly proportioned with tall, graceful windows. Magenta bougainvillaea scrambled over the creamy walls, and thick ropes of purple wisteria, dripping with delicate flowers, twined lovingly in and out of the stone balustrade edging the wide first-floor terrace. It was a dream house, set amidst lush gardens against a backcloth of mountain peaks, and facing the white-flecked, dancing sea.

The front door was opened by a short, stout man who, by reason of his deferential manner, she took to be the butler.

"Monsieur Castille is waiting for you on the terrace, Mademoiselle."

She smiled, but her heart gave a nervous jump. Monsieur Castille. That could be either Pierre or the old man.

"How is he today?" she asked as they crossed the marble-floored hall and climbed the wide, shallow stairs.

"Much better, Mademoiselle."

"I am so glad." At least she now knew it was not Pierre!

He led her through a book-lined study, out of open French windows onto the terrace. There she saw Anselm sitting in a cane chair with a huge fan-shaped back. Immediately she was struck by the frail nobility of his head with its mane of white hair and flowing beard. His high-bridged nose and pale, piercing eyes gave him the look of an ancient warrior, and, for the first time, she became aware of his resemblance to Pierre. Not so much in appearance as in demeanour—in the self-confidence, the assurance that comes with ambition, achievement and success. In Anselm it had mellowed into quiet distinction and tranquillity; in Pierre it was still a ruthless, driving force.

The artist struggled to his feet. "Willow my dear, how good of you to come down from your mountain aerie."

Willow sank into a chaise longue and the old man lowered himself into his chair. "Now my dear . . ." He picked up a drawing board to which he had already clipped a sheet of thick white paper. "I would like to make some preliminary studies before starting to paint. Tomorrow we will work in the studio. He selected a pencil from a box on the floor at his feet. "It is good to have a kind son, Willow," he said suddenly. "When you have sons I hope they will be like my Pierre."

She colored slightly and glanced away, unable to meet his eyes. Sons like Pierre indeed—no thanks! If he was kind then she was a Dutchman.

She settled herself against the cushions. "Is this all right?"

Anselm nodded. "Fine. We will not worry too much about the position today. First I must get to know your face—every bone. When I know it as well as I know my own I can begin."

He started to draw, glancing from her face to the paper with rapt concentration. How right he had been about this girl. She was the ideal subject for his brush; the small exquisitely shaped head; the high cheekbones and mobile, sensitive mouth; the creamy skin and halo of red-gold hair. In addition to her looks she radiated an inner strength coupled with an innocence which eighty years of human experience told him could only mean that no man had yet possessed her. It was a sublime moment to catch a young girl in paint: the moment before her sensual awakening.

For an hour and a half they sat in silence and complete empathy. Then Anselm put aside his work and leaned back with a sigh. "We've made an excellent start and now I am a little tired. If you will forgive me I will go and rest. You have not been bored this morning I hope?"

"Good heavens no! I have never had my portrait painted before, let alone by a famous artist. How could I be bored?"

He shot her a shrewd look from under white, furry eyebrows. "Pierre must have told you about me. What did he say exactly?"

"Nothing. I er. . . . He er . . ." she stammered.

The old man banged his hand imperiously on the arm of his chair. "Come along. I can see you are hiding something. We are friends, are we not? What did my son tell you?"

Willow hung her head miserably. "We . . . he said that you are one of the most accomplished artists in France."

Anselm snorted derisively. "Accomplished? That is a fine word to use to describe my genius! What else did he say?"

"He said . . . he said . . ." In her anxiety the words tumbled over each other. "A thousand pounds! I had no idea when I asked for that sketch . . . a thousand pounds! I didn't know, you see, or I would never have. . . . I feel so awful." Her voice trailed away to a whisper, and when she dared to glance up he was looking at her kindly.

"I see," he said quietly. "Yes, I see now." He pushed himself to his feet and came over to her. "Then I also must tell you something. It is a very long time since I have had so much pleasure from drawing anyone and I am deeply grateful. The privilege is wholly mine."

He bent down and raised her hand to his lips. "Jean will bring your lunch. *Bon appetit!*"

She watched him go in a dream. Three days ago she had been snapping her suitcase shut in Ruth's cramped bungalow and now, unbelievably, she was having her portrait painted by a renowned artist in exquisite surroundings!

"Will you take luncheon now, Mademoiselle?"

Willow jumped up. Would she! Breakfast seemed an age away.

At the far end of the terrace Jean had already covered a table with a linen cloth, antique silver cutlery and an old wine glass with a bubble threading through the stem. When she was seated he brought out a delicious meal—delicately flavoured cucumber soup followed by a light, herby omelette and a fresh green salad. She was just deciding how best to tackle a large golden peach when an attractive woman came out of the house. The first words she spoke proclaimed her American origins.

"Hi! You must be Willow. I've been hearing about you from Anselm. You've made a conquest there! How did this morning's session go?"

Her open, friendly manner put Willow at ease immediately. "Fine. I enjoyed it."

The woman smiled. "That's great. He has such hopes for the picture. By the way, I'm Arlene. I came out to see if there is anything you need."

Willow shook her head. "Nothing thanks. Everything is perfect."

"Good. My, isn't it a gorgeous day!" She

waved a beringed hand in the direction of the sea and a collection of gold bracelets tinkled expensively on her brown arm.

"Just look at that view! If only I had time to enjoy it but . . ." She consulted a tiny gold wristwatch. "I must fly. I have an appointment in Menton in fifteen minutes." She backed gracefully into the study and stood framed in the doorway, the sun glinting on her smoothly coiffured blonde hair. "I just adore this place," she breathed enthusiastically. "I can hardly bear to leave it even to go and do the shopping. Well, this won't get me to the hairdresser on time! Call Jean if you need anything." And with a final wave she was gone.

Willow sighed. Could such poise and charm be entirely a question of environment and conditioning? Most of the farmers' daughters she knew were not noted for their sophistication!

A discreet cough ended her reverie, and looking 'round she saw Jean.

"Madame Arlene said you had finished luncheon Mademoiselle, but if that is not so I can return later."

Willow stood up. "She was quite right Jean. Thank you, that was a lovely meal."

He began to clear the table and she walked back along the terrace, her mind in a turmoil. Madame Arlene said. . . . Madame Arlene . . . Madame . . . The words echoed in her head. She must be Pierre's wife! Somehow he had not given the impression of being married. But why not? It would be surprising if a rich, personable, cultured man in his mid-thirties were not married. And in Arlene he had obviously found the perfect mate: an elegant, attractive woman—worldly but good-natured. They probably had a brood of fascinating children tucked away in the nurseries of Villa Martine, watched over by an English nanny.

She had just begun to descend the stone staircase to the garden when a familiar figure suddenly dashed 'round the corner and started to leap up the steps two at a time. An involuntary "Oh!" escaped her lips. He stopped short and looked up, shielding his eyes against the sun.

"I thought you had gone."

So he had been avoiding her! "I am going now," she said, keeping her voice light and cool.

He continued to mount the steps until he reached her level. "I am sorry if I startled you."

"You didn't," she lied.

His mouth twitched with amusement. "That's all right then."

"Well, only a little," she confessed shyly.

He pointed an accusing finger. "I think you are compulsively honest! Am I right?"

"Yes, you are," she said looking directly into his eyes.

He nodded slowly. "I thought so."

So it was over. He believed her. He no longer thought she was a fortune-hunting adventuress. Yesterday's nightmare had ended. She felt quite dizzy with relief.

"How do you think my father looks?" he asked confidentially.

"Frail."

"But content yes? I mean he is not yearning for his own home?"

Willow shook her head. "No. Anyway I agree with you he is not well enough to go back to the village."

A rare, warm smile lit his face. "I am glad we agree. It is thanks to you he is staying here."

"To me?"

"Of course to you. Who else?" He moved down a step. "Come, we will walk to your car and you can tell me how my obstinate old father has ruined your holiday plans."

"But he hasn't," she protested as they descended together. "I really enjoy sitting for him. And your house is so lovely, and everyone is so kind—your father, Arlene . . ."

"So you have met Arlene. That's good."

"Yes. She's delightful and so attractive."

"Naturally." He sounded surprised. "We Castilles are renowned for our magnificent women."

She glanced at him to see if he was joking, but his face was serious. The old irritation flared briefly. Of course the Castilles would pride themselves on their women—on all their possessions no doubt!

They walked slowly across the manicured lawns towards the drive.

"What are you going to do when you are not sitting for the portrait?" he asked.

"I intend to explore the countryside around Colombaia," Willow said, her voice quickening with anticipation. "I'm hoping to identify as many species of flora as possible. It's a golden opportunity. Perhaps I'll come across something really rare."

"So, you are a botanist?"

She laughed. "Nothing so grand. I am a florist."

"I see. And will you go on these expeditions alone?"

"Naturally."

"I am sorry but I must forbid it."

Willow stopped walking, her face a picture of amazement.

"I don't understand." Perhaps she had not heard correctly.

"You can't go alone," he said calmly, "and I'm too busy to accompany you."

"I didn't ask you to accompany me!" Just who did he think he was, ordering her about like this? For a few minutes he had seemed so gentle and friendly—a different man from the one she had come to expect. But leopards don't change their spots; she had been a fool to imagine this one had!

"You cannot go," he repeated.

"But why on earth not?"

He looked at her as if she was extremely stupid. "Because it isn't safe of course."

She laughed scornfully. "Not safe? I didn't know you still had bandits in this part of France!"

He assumed an air of weary patience. "Don't be deliberately obtuse. The mountain paths are treacherous. There are dangerous patches of scree everywhere. You could fall and injure yourself."

Willow tapped her foot impatiently on the grass. "I am not a total idiot. I have come across scree before, you know."

"Perhaps. But you don't know this country. You could easily get lost. It might be difficult to find you."

She gave him a sweet smile. "Well, if I do perhaps you will lead the search party unless"— she paused mischievously—"unless you are too busy of course."

"You are behaving like a spoilt child," he said roughly.

"And you are behaving like a . . . like a . . ."

He arched an eyebrow. "Husband?"

"Schoolmaster!" she finished furiously.

For ten seconds they glared at each other, then Willow ran across the grass towards her car.

"You would be wise to take my advice," he called.

Without looking back she wrenched open the door, flung herself into the driving seat, started the engine and roared along the avenue of trees and out of the gates as fast as she dared.

"Darn you and your advice, Pierre Castille!" she fumed. "Whose holiday is this anyway?"

Angrily snatching her sun glasses off the map-shelf, she slammed them on to her nose. If she hurried she could be back in Colombaia in time to set out on her first expedition. She must show these Castilles once and for all that they did not own her and could not tell her what to do or what not to do. She was not one of their elegant, expensive possessions. She belonged exclusively to herself, and that was the way it was going to stay!

Willow slid the car into a parking space and crossed the square to her favorite lookout-spot. The weather was perfect. Not a cloud marred the cerulean sky, a silver sea gleamed on the horizon, and although the sun was hot a tempering breeze played with her hair and cooled her skin. Satisfied, she turned and walked briskly across the square to the passage leading to the Rue des Fleurs.

Entering the little house she changed into jeans, T shirt and walking shoes. She threw a few essentials into a red nylon satchel and clattered downstairs into the sunshine.

The dull clang of the church bell chimed out across the village. Five o'clock: a little on the late side, but there was still plenty of time before the sun began to sink behind the mountain and the air grow chill. Instead of following the usual route she took a short cut, a track dipping down to the road between modest gardens crowded with vigorous vegetables, bright marigolds and tall poppies with dark velvety centers.

When she reached the road she remembered that she had left the map of the district lying on the kitchen table. She paused uncertainly; she ought to return for it but the climb back to the house would waste precious time. The path she wanted started beyond the village outskirts and wound down the mountainside to a tiny mysterious settlement which appeared to be surrounded by footpaths but had no road. It shouldn't be difficult to find, and it would be fascinating to meet people still living in so isolated a situation yet so close, as the crow flew, to a large town like Menton.

An old Frenchman with a wrinkled, prune-like face was sitting on the parapet at the edge of the road. Willow gave him a friendly smile as she passed and received a brief, dour nod in return. After walking a hundred or so meters she turned aside from the wide dusty road onto the track she had spotted on the map. It dropped steeply down the mountain, twisting and turning until the distant vista of Menton and the sea disappeared and she found herself in a gentle jungle of grass and flowers. Pungent smells of earth and flowers assailed her nostrils as she picked her way over the rough ground and waded through heavily scented bromme grass and golden gorse. But her progress, although delightful, was slow and after a while her head began to feel heavy and her eyelids began to droop. She knew that if she sat down she would go to sleep and reluctantly decided to defer all botanical study until the return journey.

Even so, coming unexpectedly upon a fruit-laden cherry tree mysteriously surrounded by a crumbling wall, she broke her resolve and scrambled over the wall. The sweet juicy fruit revived her and after feasting liberally she sank down to rest in the shade. The heady odors of the sun-baked mountain enveloped her and somewhere nearby she thought she could hear the sound of running water. Cool . . . cool . . . with a contented sigh she leaned back against the trunk of the old tree. . . .

She awoke with a start, slightly chilled and extremely annoyed with herself for dropping off. It was seven o'clock. The scene had altered dramatically. Instead of a bright sunny day it was now overcast and a familiar pall of mist shrouded the landscape.

Jumping to her feet she climbed back over the wall and set off at a brisk pace. The sound of water, proving a reality, gradually grew louder until she was sure there must be a waterfall nearby. The narrow path unexpectedly widened into long shallow steps similar to the ones in Colombaia, but slippery and treacherous with loose stones. Deeper and deeper it plunged through a tunnel of twisting, stunted trees whose claw-like branches grasped each other fiercely above her head. The dense creepers clothing the tree trunks and clinging to the banks each side of the path added to the dank gloom and she hurried on, half-tempted to turn back, a nasty suspicion beginning to nag at the back of her mind.

When the first ruined dwellings loomed out of the mist her misgivings were confirmed. The mystery village was nothing but a collection of abandoned crofts, only inhabited by animals and birds. No one had lived there for years.

Disappointed, but fascinated, she wandered in and out of the weather-ravaged crofts trying to picture them in better days, when thick stone walls fitted snugly under slate roofs and grassy plots were crowded with grunting pigs and cackling hens. It must have been a hard life. The men must have had to walk a long way to find work; the women would have hauled provisions up steep footpaths from the town in all weathers—an increasingly difficult way of life in a modern world. In the end it obviously defeated them and they packed up their possessions and departed. Inevitable but sad.

The mist, sweeping in from the sea, rose and fell on the breath of a fresh breeze, manipulating the landscape like a child playing with a toy theater. For minutes at a time she could clearly see the layout of the village—crofts with four walls but no roof, windows gaping like empty tooth sockets in the mouth of an old man, lichen-covered water tanks half-hidden by creepers and waist-high weeds. A desolate sight but for the thousands of pink and mauve briar roses rioting everywhere, softening the harsh outlines of decay and devastation.

She had been right about the stream; it rushed and foamed exuberantly through the middle of the village spanned by a sturdy iron bridge. Succumbing to temptation she crossed it but the stony steps soon turned into a steep narrow track and after climbing for twenty minutes through thick mist she decided to call it a day.

Cautiously she began to descend the path but the fog surged towards her reducing the visibility to a few meters. The atmosphere, dream-like and unreal until that moment, suddenly felt oppressive, and she quickened her steps.

Coming to a division in the path she automatically turned right, expecting any minute to arrive at the iron bridge. But although she could hear the stream gushing over the rocks nearby, the bridge failed to appear. Generally she was so observant; it was ridiculous to start imagining she was lost. After all, there had only been one track winding down the mountain. Or had there? What about all the other footpaths marked on the map? Dozens of them. It would be easy to take the wrong one and find herself walking into the hills instead of back to Colombaia.

Her confidence, already undermined, began to falter. Within a few minutes the sound of water died away and she knew with a sinking heart that she had definitely taken the wrong turning. Admonishing herself to keep calm she steadily retraced her steps, but the mist had settled heavily into the trees and she could not even find the point where she had made the first mistake.

She wandered helplessly on, the ghostly vapor swirling about her. What ought she to do, press forward or wait until the mist lifted? Even then there was no guarantee that she would be able to find the right path unless . . . She stopped and strained to listen. Thank heavens! The stream again. Deliberately she left the path, pushed impatiently through the dense bushes and stumbled downhill towards the sound.

Gradually the ground leveled out, and before long she walked into a grassy clearing surrounded by a broken-down wall. She could have shouted with joy. She was back in the village. In her relief she began to run, tossed her satchel over the low wall and lightheartedly leapt after it.

Her cry of alarm as she found herself falling through space caused a large bird to squawk noisily and flap away through the trees. Her subsequent cry of pain went unheeded by animals and birds alike.

Chapter Four

The world exploded into a million stars. For a long time she lay still, too stunned by shock and fright to move. After an eternity the breath returned to her body with a deep shuddering gasp and her brain began to function again. There was an excruciating pain in her left ankle. What on earth had happened? Bewildered, she looked around for an explanation, then let out an exasperated groan. How could she have been daft enough to jump blindly over a wall and drop eight or ten feet onto a hard path? Pierre's fears had been fully justified; if he heard about the incident he would probably die laughing. Tears of self-pity blurred her vision but she forced them back. Crying would not help. Carefully she sat up, put her right foot on the ground and stood on it.

Testing her weight on her left foot, she yelped and sat down again. It was no good; she could not possibly walk.

Around her the mist hung in a gray vaporous blanket. She looked at her watch. Eight-fifteen. At a rough guess she had about forty-five minutes before dark to make her way home. Less perhaps. Spurred on by anxiety, she propelled herself along the ground to retrieve her satchel which had fallen into the undergrowth. Groping for it she caught the dull gleam of water at the foot of the slope below the path. The stream! If she could reach it and soak her ankle in the cold water she might be able to hobble along with the aid of a stick.

She began to awkwardly inch down the slope on all fours. The going was rough, the descent precarious and every movement agony. Once, knocking her leg against the rotting branch of a fallen tree, she nearly fainted. A wave of nausea engulfed her but she made herself breathe deeply until it passed.

Gaining the stream she lowered her foot into the bubbling water and kept it immersed as long as she could bear, but when she withdrew it the swelling was bluish, puffier than before, and the pain was acute. Again she consulted her watch. Eight-forty-five. It was useless to sit and wait to be rescued; no one knew where she had gone. She would not be missed until she failed to arrive for her portrait session the next day. Even then Pierre would probably ascribe her absence to their last argument! Her heart skipped a beat and a sensation uncomfortably close to panic fluttered in her chest. To distract herself she watched a water vole scuttle past and plunge into the stream then, scooping up a handful of water, splashed her face and sat back to think calmly.

She must do something. The thought of spending the night on the open mountain was terrifying. It would be more sensible to look for shelter while it was still light. Suddenly, she remembered a croft situated in the center of the village street on the far side of the stream. It lacked only a door and a window and was snug and dry inside. If she could find it again she would be assured of reasonable protection through the dark hours ahead, and at dawn she could resume the homeward trail.

First she had to cross the stream, a more formidable task at close range than at first sight. About ten meters wide, flowing fast along a rocky bed, it continually dropped away in a series of small weirs formed by boulders over which the water gushed and foamed at an alarming rate, presenting a daunting obstacle to safety.

Hanging the satchel 'round her neck she cautiously entered the icy water which surged over her, threatening to knock her off her feet. Desperately she clung to the nearest rock, horribly tempted to give up and allow her tired body to be swept away like a heap of useless debris. Every time she released her hold on the slippery surface the churning waters upset her balance and she was forced to lunge out and grab another mooring. Her aching ankle forgotten, she kept strug-

gling forward, grasping at anything firmly
anchored—spindly young trees, weeds, anything!
Suddenly she stepped into a deep clear pool and,
sinking quickly, felt the water close over her
head. Instinctively she pushed herself up from the
river bed with both feet and a crippling pain shot
through her ankle. She yelled and was instantly
swept downstream by the frothy, buffeting water.
Over and over she tumbled, impotently lashing
out with her arms and legs in an effort to gain
control of the situation. When she finally bobbed
to the surface, choking for air, she found herself
washed up against a massive boulder only a meter
or two from the bank. Thankfully she crawled
clear of the stream and collapsed shivering on the
grass.

After a few minutes she pushed herself onto
her hands and knees and started to crawl up the
steep bank. She could see nothing but dense mist
and hear nothing but the roar of the water below.
A bleak sensation of utter loneliness came over
her. It could be days, weeks before she was
discovered. Oh why hadn't she gone back for the
wretched map? Stupid, stupid, stupid! Slowly but
surely her fear and despair turned to anger: a
healthy anger, a cleansing anger which began to
generate a grim determination to survive.

Summoning all her reserves of strength she
heaved her unwilling body up the slope, gradually
gaining the summit, and as she crouched there
wondering where to go next, an auspicious breeze
briefly lifted the curtain of mist revealing the very
croft she had visualized down by the stream.

Slowly, painfully, she covered the short distance and crawled through the open doorway.

The croft was surprisingly warm, stuffy even. Stripping off her wet shirt she wrung it out and suspended it from a projecting nail in the wall. She then tried to wriggle out of her jeans but discovered she could not ease the leg over her swollen foot. What a ridiculous mess! She was so tired, and her ankle ached. . . .

Kneeling gently over onto the floor of the little croft, Willow closed her eyes.

The pain awoke her, throbbing like an Indian tom-tom in her ankle. She was immediately aware of being hungry, cold and stiff. Instinct told her it was well past midnight. The mist had obligingly lifted but the sky was a mass of turbulent clouds chasing across the indigo heavens in pursuit of some unimaginable quarry. In an hour or two it would start to grow light and she could begin to find her way home.

Her shirt and jeans were still wet but she would have to pull them on before starting out. Even so her knees and hands were bound to suffer badly during the crawl up the mountain. She drew a long tremulous breath. No, she would not cry! Crying never cured anything.

The sharp, unmistakable cracking of dry twigs suddenly made her scalp prickle. Something or someone was approaching the croft. A wild animal perhaps? She held her breath and cast vainly 'round the croft for something to lay across the entrance but there was nothing. Huddling fearfully against the wall she waited, her heart ready to leap out of her throat.

A brilliant beam of light fell across the doorway.

"Who is it? *Qui va là?*" she croaked.

The light whirled 'round, thrust into the dark room and pinned her into the corner blinding her with its glare. Instinctively she raised both hands to shield her eyes and a familiar voice, strained with emotion exclaimed, "*Mon Dieu! C'est toi!* It really is you, Willow? Are you all right?"

Throwing herself forward she clung to him, sobbing with relief. "Pierre! Thank heavens you have come. I have been so frightened. I can't walk because my ankle hurts and I am so cold!"

Silently, rhythmically he rocked her in his arms while the terror and frustration of the past hours expended itself in a torrent of woe.

When her sobs had died down to the occasional bone-shaking hiccough Pierre sat her gently on the floor.

"Am I correct in thinking you have recently had pneumonia?"

She nodded, still unable to speak.

"Then we must get you warm." Peeling off his sweater he pulled it over her head and pushed her arms into the sleeves like a father dressing his small child. Then he went outside for a moment and returned with a knapsack from which he quickly extracted a vacuum flask and a light blanket.

"I c-can't get my jeans off," complained Willow

through chattering teeth. "They are soaking w-wet but won't go over my foot."

Taking up the injured foot he examined it carefully. "Can you move it?"

She tried but winced with pain. "Only a little. Do you think it is broken?"

Again he ran his hands over the swelling. "I don't think so but I can't be sure. It must be X-rayed." He pulled a sheathed knife out of the knapsack. "I will have to cut away the leg of your jeans."

With a single stroke of the razor-sharp blade he freed her foot and wrapped the blanket 'round her legs. "Now that's more comfortable, humm?" Putting away the knife he poured her a drink from the flask. "You must get this inside you. It is strong coffee and cognac."

While she sipped the scalding, aromatic drink he again dived into the bag and produced a bar of chocolate and a packet of tablets. "Take two of these with the coffee. They will help the pain."

Willow's eyes grew round with astonishment. "But how did you know I would need all these things?"

"You are not the first person to disappear on this mountain," he said drily. "Some were lucky but others were found many months later—what was left of them. Now you know why I didn't want you to go!"

"I still don't understand. How did you know where I'd gone? How did you find me?"

He grinned, a lopsided expression caused by the dragging scar on his cheek. "When you left my house yesterday I knew exactly what you meant to do."

She hung her head, ashamed to look at him. "It was stupid of me. I . . . I . . ."

"It's finished," he broke in, "you will not do such a thing again."

"But I have given you so much trouble."

"Indeed you have. But I ought to have made you understand the danger. Perhaps I should have locked you in my cellar to stop you!"

This good-humored sally failed to induce a smile mainly because she thought him perfectly capable of carrying out the threat.

"Anyway," he continued, "I decided to give you plenty of time to get over your temper and then follow you. However things rarely work out as we would like and as I was getting into the car a business client arrived in urgent need of advice. I couldn't get away for hours and by the time I finally reached your house you had left."

Willow closed her cold hands around the coffee cup, grateful for the penetrating warmth. "What then?"

He looked at her severely. "Then I should have returned to my villa and minded my own business. Is that not so?"

She nodded dumbly.

"But," he continued lightly, "I naturally felt I had to uphold the tradition of all gallant Frenchmen and save a rash woman from the results of her own foolishness."

This was more like the Pierre she knew! "So what did you decide to do?"

"I did what every other sensible man would have done. I joined my friend Armand Leduc in a glass of wine at his hotel."

"I see." She lowered her eyes to hide her chagrin.

He chuckled. "Now you are cross. You think I—how shall I put it?—You think that I fiddled while Rome was burning? Do you not understand that two heads are better than one? There are many paths into the hills from Colombaia. The difficulty was guessing which one you had chosen. It was Anna Leduc who suggested consulting Raoul Guerat."

"Who is he?"

Pierre laughed, his white teeth gleaming in the darkness. "Raoul knows everything. For thirty years he has sat outside his house all day watching people come and go."

"Of course!" She exclaimed. "I remember now. I passed him coming out of the village. Doesn't he have to work or anything?"

"Raoul work? He was wounded in the war and received a full disability pension. He has never been known to lift a finger to earn money since. Naturally he was able to tell me that he had seen you come this way but had not seen you return."

Willow snuggled deeper into his soft sweater which smelled faintly and pleasantly of lemons. "And after that?"

"After that I returned to the hotel, put together a few things and, although you did not deserve it, I set off to find you. I have known these hills all my life and thought you would make straight for

Villette. Unfortunately I had no idea how far you had strayed from the path, or if you had deliberately taken a different route back to the village. After crossing the bridge I walked for about an hour without finding a trace of you but on my way back I spotted something odd lying up on the bank under the bridge. It was this." Plunging his hand into another pocket of the knapsack he pulled out her soggy satchel and handed it over.

"Yes this is mine." she said.

"After finding that I decided to search the whole place before going any farther."

He stopped speaking and the soft soughing of the wind in the trees filled the silence as they gazed at each other across the beam of torchlight.

"I don't know how to thank . . ." she began.

"Hush." Leaning over, he placed a finger against her lips. "Then say nothing."

Willow shook her head. "I have been so thoughtless, so pig-headed. . . ."

He nodded gravely. "I cannot deny it but . . ." He snapped his fingers in the air, "Now it's forgotten. Agreed?"

She swallowed the rising lump in her throat. "All right."

"Good." He began to repack the haversack. "Now we must think how to get you back."

"It'll be a long crawl," she predicted.

He looked up sharply. "Crawl did you say? Were you intending to crawl all the way back to Colombaia?"

"Of course. How else can I get there? I certainly can't walk."

He shook his head at the absurdity of the notion. "You would never make it. Your hands and knees would be raw before you covered half the distance."

"What do you suggest then? Can you teach me to fly?"

The joke fell on stony ground. "We have two alternatives," he said seriously. "Either I leave you here and go for help—"

"No!" Her voice rose in alarm. "Please don't leave me alone Pierre. Please!"

"Then I shall have to carry you," he said matter-of-factly.

Willow looked aghast. "Carry me? You can't mean it!"

His eyes travelled calculatingly over her body. "How much do you weigh? Fifty kilos?"

"A hundred and ten pounds but you can't possibly . . ."

He silenced her with an authoritative gesture. "You are in no position to judge. We'll do as I say." He glanced out of the door. "The weather is very unsettled but we must risk it. You can ride piggyback to start with. I'm afraid it won't be comfortable and you must hang on, but please don't strangle me!"

The ghost of a smile flickered across her white face. "I'll try not to." Oddly enough she felt ready to undertake the journey. She was warm at last and the pain had receded to a dull ache.

Pierre threw the knapsack into a corner. "I can return for our things later."

He helped her outside and, draping the blanket

'round her shoulders, tied the ends together like a shawl. "You can't wear your wet clothes but this will protect you from the cold."

For the first time she was acutely aware of her tiny cotton pants. If she had been given a glimpse of the future she might well have invested in a pair of bloomers with elastic 'round the knees!

Kneeling on the ground Pierre told her to climb astride his back. Clumsily, she did so, holding onto the wall of the croft for support. He grasped her legs, allowing her feet to dangle freely, and levered himself to a standing position.

"When you get too tired we'll rest," he promised. *"Tout va bien?"*

"Fine." She glanced down. The ground seemed a long way off.

"Good. Then we go."

He set off at a brisk walk, threading his way expertly between loose rocks and trailing brambles while Willow tried to make herself as light as possible.

High above them boiling storm clouds gradually obliterated the remaining pockets of starry sky. The gusting wind propelled Pierre on and up the steep track. Willow leaned forward like a jockey intent on winning a race, and felt the muscles in his waist and back contract between her thighs as he leapt ahead, nimble as a mountain goat.

"We must hurry—it's going to rain heavily," he said, raising his voice above the wind.

As he spoke the first drops splashed onto her nose followed thick and fast by others. Soon the path was awash and Pierre, head down, squelched doggedly on through a blinding sheet of water which soon began to flood down the track over his feet carrying with it a small avalanche of sticks and stones. Twice he slipped and nearly fell but saved himself by slithering backwards, arms outstretched to keep his precarious balance. Slowly, resolutely, bent almost double, he regained the lost ground and plodded on through the deluge.

A flash of lightning, brighter than the brightest sunlight, lit up the mountain and Willow cowered down, pressing her face into his shoulder.

He turned his head. "You're scared?"

"A little."

Pierre lifted his streaming face to the punishing sky. "Storms are marvelous—an unchanging, unchangeable part of our heritage. Listen."

She listened to the low, rumbling thunder rolling majestically around the mountain peaks.

"The voice of the great god Jupiter," Pierre said.

"When he is angry he roars his displeasure."

Another flash of lightning zigzagged up the mountainside followed by an earsplitting crack of thunder. Willow gave a little cry, and slid to the ground where she huddled covering her face with her hands.

"I can't go on! I can't!"

Immediately he dropped to his haunches. "It's all right," he soothed, pushing her wet hair back from her face. "We must keep going. Trust me." Dragging her hands away from her terrified face he forced her to look at him. "You must trust me."

His hair was plastered to his forehead and his mouth grim, but his eyes—clear, blue and utterly compelling—gave her the courage she needed, and she nodded quickly.

He untied the sodden blanket 'round her neck and let it fall. Swinging her up in his arms he proceeded to carry her up the mountain as if she were no more than an awkward parcel he was late in posting.

Mercifully the rain gradually slackened to a drizzle and the thunder ceased although the lightning continued to flicker spasmodically, like a sullen child unwilling to go away and play somewhere else.

At last the ramparts of the village came into view and Pierre clambered onto a grassy hummock and put her down in the sheltering lee of a boulder. He was breathing heavily but gave no other sign of undue fatigue.

Silently he pointed to the east. Dawn was breaking over the sea. A pink crack, edged with bronze, slowly split open the gray horizon. As they watched, it grew wider—the pink deepening to flame-red until the sky was a fiery, kaleidoscopic mass merging with the reflecting aluminum sea. Above them the sloping roofs of Colombaia took on strong roseate hues and the pallid rock face of the mountain upon which the village rested became streaked with crimson and stained dark with patches of scrubby bushes.

Willow held her breath. An unexpected, almost unearthly happiness possessed her. It was as if her whole life had led to this moment; as if she were experiencing a vision of perfection which could never be destroyed by any pain or grief she might suffer later. It was a moment to treasure for as long as she lived, a moment shared with a magnetic stranger who, quite suddenly, seemed as familiar to her as her own soul.

" 'Bliss it was in that dawn to be alive.' " Willow quoted.

" 'But to be young was very Heaven,' " Pierre concluded quietly.

She started, unaware that she had spoken aloud. "I had forgotten the last bit."

"Wordsworth was writing about France. You like France I think."

"Oh, I do!" She hugged her knees with pleasure.

"Good. So do I." He stood up. "Now we will go home." Bending down he gathered her in his arms again and striding along easily soon covered the short distance to the village.

"Will Raoul Guerat be watching from his window?" Willow asked nervously.

Pierre grinned. "Of course."

"But what will he think, seeing you carrying a half-naked girl?"

"You're not so naked. You're wearing my best sweater."

"But I have nothing on my legs."

He laughed. "Raoul will enjoy the sight immensely. We must not deprive him of pleasure by passing his house too quietly. After all if it were not for him you might still be at the bottom of the mountain. Let's sing for him. You must know this song too." Throwing back his head, he sang: *"Il pleut, il pleut bergère . . ."* His rich baritone rang out in the morning air.

Willow laughed. *"Il ron, ron, ron, petit pat-a-pon,"* she warbled.

A puzzled, grizzled face appeared at the Guerat window and Pierre waved cheerfully at Raoul.

Chapter Five

As they were nearing Number Nine Willow lifted a dismayed face up to her rescuer. "We can't get in—the key is in my satchel."

"We'll soon find another," he promised, and setting her down on a ledge he groped under a stone near the door. *"Voilà!* What did I tell you?" He waved the key triumphantly. "Until the tourists came no one ever bothered to lock up. It is, after all, a most inconvenient arrangement."

He carried her upstairs and put her down on a chair in the bedroom then he disappeared into the adjoining bathroom and emerged a minute later in a cloud of steam. "I should take you straight to the hospital but first you must have a warm bath. I don't think you've broken anything but I can't be sure. We must gamble on it. A hot bath is the quickest way to avoid a chill."

Willow shook her head obstinately. "I don't want a bath. I just want to sleep."

"Well that's too bad," he said, and lifting her up he carried her into the bathroom and sat her on the edge of the bathtub.

"Arms up!" He ordered.

Wearily she obeyed.

He pulled off the borrowed sweater and then turned his back. "Take off the rest of your clothes and I'll help you get into the bath."

A slow blush crept up her neck to her hair. "That won't be necessary. I can manage alone."

"Fine." Leaning against the doorpost he gazed steadfastly away into the bedroom. "Then get on with it."

With cold, numb fingers she struggled to undo her brassiere, wriggled out of her pants and, sliding backwards, vanished beneath the foaming, perfumed water.

She surfaced choking and spluttering, to find Pierre, arms akimbo, laughing down at her.

"That was an amusing little trick. Do you know any others?"

Grabbing the soap she flung it at him. "Go away!"

Still laughing he retreated through the open door. "Next time perhaps you'll let me help you!"

She glared at him over the billowing froth.

"I promise to keep my eyes closed," he said.

"I can manage," she repeated firmly. It wasn't only his eyes she was worried about!

"Very well, then I'll make some coffee."

"Pierre . . ." The husky, contrite voice stopped him before he reached the landing.

"Yes?"

"You think I am an awful prude don't you?"

"A prude?" He considered the word as if he had never heard it before. "A prude, no. But I think you are sometimes rather silly."

Willow lay back in the bath, relaxing in the hot water. So he thought her silly, did he? True, she had acted incredibly foolishly but he didn't have to keep harping on it. He obviously enjoyed putting her at a disadvantage, and making her feel awkward and naive. She sighed. Whatever the result of the X-ray, her holiday was now ruined. She couldn't walk, couldn't even drive. If she telephoned home for advice she would immediately be told to take the first flight back to England. There must be another way. . . .

At that point her exhausted mind gave up the fight. It was hard enough coping with the present without trying to juggle with the future. Instead she gazed contentedly around the jade green bathroom with its fluffy beige towels and glass containers of bath essence. Every comfort had been provided, even to a bathrobe hanging on the back of the door. Looking at it she was suddenly struck by the thought that she knew nothing about the owners of the house. They must be kind people; the rent was amazingly reasonable. If she had to go home earlier than planned she would still feel bound to pay it. The whole thing seemed such a waste.

A delicious aroma of coffee, wafting through from the bedroom, announced Pierre's return. She heard him put down the tray.

"Are you ready to get out?"

"Not yet." In no way was she going to ask for help! Grasping the sides of the bath she tried to heave herself upright on her good leg but slipped and fell back with a resounding splash.

In seconds he was at the side of the bath. "You can be very contrary," he fumed. "I told you to call me."

"I can manage," she insisted sulkily.

With barely suppressed irritation he released the bath water, whipped the robe off the door and held it out. "Put this on."

It was no time to argue! Submissively she allowed him to lift her out of the bath, and she quickly slid her arms into the large sleeves.

He carried her into the bedroom, put her down on the bed and, fetching a towel from the bathroom, pressed her head to his flat stomach and began to dry her hair with slow rhythmical movements. At the same time he chanted an old folk song in a strange guttural patois. Willow closed her eyes and relaxed against his body, lulled by the soothing hands and melancholy little tune.

"What do the words mean?" she asked when it ended.

"The marguerites in the fields are not so fair as your skin, nor the poppies so red as your lips. Shall I pluck them or leave them alone?" Standing back he surveyed her flushed cheeks. "Something like that anyway." He flicked the end of her nose lightly with his finger. "You're looking better. Drink your coffee while I have a quick shower to remove all this mud."

While he was in the bathroom she sipped the coffee and listened to Colombaia's cockerels crowing in leisurely succession. Below in the valley an old car was noisily grinding up the steep road to the village. A new day had begun. Putting down the cup, she lay back on the pillow, sighed deeply and at once fell into a sound sleep.

When she awoke the sun was casting ribs of golden light through the shutters onto the floor. Her ankle still throbbed horribly. Turning over she saw Pierre, half-wrapped in a towel, asleep on the far side of the bed. Raising herself on one elbow she gazed curiously down at him. His long, tanned limbs, although perfectly relaxed, looked ready to spring into action at the first warning. His arms and legs were sprinkled with fine dark hairs but his chest was smooth and his lean, muscular body boasted not an ounce of spare flesh. He lay sprawled out in a sleep of sheer fatigue and, for the first time, she became aware of how much the night's events must have cost him in pure physical effort. No wonder he was exhausted. Even when they reached the house his thoughts had been entirely for her safety and comfort.

She leaned closer. Asleep he appeared younger than when awake. The harsh lines in his face melted away, the bitter mouth relaxed and the tousled hair falling across his forehead made him look more like a boy of her own age than a man in his thirties. The only blemish was the deep, disfiguring scar on his cheek. Hardly conscious of moving, she reached out and ran her finger lightly along the ugly jagged line. Instantly the blue eyes flew open and before she had time to draw back she was in his arms, her body pinioned to his, her lips eagerly responding to his importunate, seeking mouth.

A tingling, burning sensation, starting at the base of her spine, spread swiftly through her veins until her whole being seemed to fuse with his in an all-consuming fire. Her fingers, endowed with a will of their own, urgently kneaded his naked, sleep-warmed shoulders and entwined themselves in the thick, crisp hair at the back of his head. She felt him slip his hand inside her robe and the immediate response of her breasts to his touch jolted her to an awareness of the heat of their mounting passion. With a frightened little gasp she jerked away and rolled over to the far side of the bed.

He let her go, merely staring at her with heavy-lidded, aroused eyes. "I see. As a tease I would rate you first-class. Expert in fact."

"If you think that . . ." she began hotly.

"Then you had better fasten your robe."

Appalled, she clutched at the open robe, pulled it around her and retied the sash tightly.

The Frenchman's long mobile lips curled into an insolent smile. "You are just a little girl. For a while I did not believe it but it is true. A little English miss who should still be playing with her dolls."

Confused by his change of mood she regarded him warily, her alarmed green eyes, trembling mouth and wild tangle of red-gold hair lending her the air of a dryad ready to dart into the forest at the first note of the huntsman's horn.

"If you mean that I am prim and inexperienced . . ." she said, hardly able to hear her own voice above the drumming of her heart.

"That is not what I said."

"But it is what you meant."

The blue eyes regarded her with amusement. "When a beautiful girl studies me for a long time and then strokes my cheek with her pretty finger . . ."

Willow's face flamed. Of all the mean tricks! He had been awake all the time. She sat up abruptly and would have eased herself off the bed if he had not caught her arm.

"Where do you think you are going?"

"To dress," she replied shortly.

He still held on. "No. You're running away. I believe you're frightened of the woman you really are."

She swung 'round to face him, her eyelids snapping angrily. "Really? Well, whatever kind of woman you believe I am it is definitely not the kind who plays around with married men!"

"Married men?" His mouth twitched with amusement. "What makes you think I am married?"

"But I thought . . ."

He shook his head in mock reproval. "You don't always think. That's one of your problems."

She had been about to say that she thought Arlene, the American, was his wife when the bald truth suddenly dawned. She was not his wife but his mistress. Of course! What a fool she had been not to see it before. A man like Pierre—rich, successful and attractive—would inevitably have a current favorite. Recalling Arlene's friendly, open manner Willow was seized with outrage. Who said it was no longer a man's world? Women were still pawns in the sex game—toyed with for their youth, beauty, money or position and discarded at their master's convenience. Well, it was never going to happen to her!

"Isn't it time we left for the hospital?" she asked briskly.

"Of course. Whenever you wish." He released her arm and dropped his legs over the side of the bed. "But first I must pack your valise so that you can return with me to Villa Martine."

"Go home with you?" Could he be serious?

"Naturally. What else can you do?"

"But that's impossible."

"Impossible? How so? It's a very simple matter."

How could she explain? What excuse could she give without sounding like a character in a Victorian novel? Anyway he was right. What else could she do? Even if there were no broken bones she would not be able to move around unaided for several days. How would she obtain food? How pass the time? Even so she could not take advantage of his offer. She had caused enough trouble already.

"I think I'd better return to England as soon as possible," she said reluctantly.

He stood up. "Then you're willing to disappoint my father?"

Anselm and the portrait! She had forgotten her promise to the old man. Poor Anselm, he was counting on her. Perhaps she could just stay until her actual presence was no longer required—say a week at the most.

Pierre picked up his clothes and strolled to the door. "He will need the rest of your holiday," he said casually as he went out.

Willow hopped painfully over to the chest and tugged crossly at a drawer. It was not the first time that this arrogant but perceptive man had read her thoughts. The very last thing she wanted was to stay at the villa with him and his mistress. She would feel trapped and miserable and thoroughly *de trop*.

Resentfully she threw her blue silk shirt onto a chair.

A hospital porter produced a wheel chair and the examination was carried out quickly and efficiently. "No," the doctor said, "the ankle was not broken, it was merely badly wrenched. In a few days the swelling would go down, until then take pain pills every four hours."

The doctor scribbled an address where they could pick up a pair of crutches for Willow to use temporarily and hurried away, his mind already occupied with weightier matters.

They drove back via the sea front. The sun dancing on the water set Willow's heart dancing too. Despite the complications of the past twenty-four hours and the apprehension with which she viewed the immediate future, she was still charmed by the glorious day—the light playing on the mellow buildings of the old town, the cafés and the relaxed mood of the people shopping or just sitting in the squares under gaily striped umbrellas.

"Isn't it all heavenly!" she exclaimed.

Pierre glanced sideways at her, touched by her pleasure. "You're happy that your ankle is not serious," he said.

"I suppose I am. Yes, that must be it."

Lifting his hand off the wheel he placed it lightly on the nape of her neck. "I'm happy too."

Willow stared straight ahead. Her neck burned under his fingers. Would she never be able to meet these friendly, innocuous gestures with an equally unaffected response?

He nosed the Ferrari into the driveway of Villa Martine. "I hope you won't be too bored here. Jean and his wife, Nicole, will look after you and of course, you'll have my father for company. Unfortunately I have to go away on business for a few days but I'm leaving you in good hands."

The bright day suddenly turned dark with disappointment and she could not trust herself to reply.

"I daresay you won't mind too much," her host commented drily, switching off the engine.

She longed to say, I mind very much. Must you really go? But instead she murmured something noncommittal as she opened the car door.

Jean, hovering in the drive in response to Pierre's telephone call, bore away her suitcase and Willow transferred her attention to managing the crutches. Tartly declining Pierre's help she negotiated the distance between the car and the house with tolerable ease. The long flight of stone steps however was a different matter. Clumsily she hoisted herself up the first few steps and paused to rest.

"Lean on me," offered Pierre.

"I can manage, thanks."

"Right." He fell in behind her. "Go ahead then."

Slowly she pulled her reluctant body up seven more steps, her arms aching with the effort. Her tormentor followed saying. "Why are you taking so long? I thought you were an expert."

Beads of perspiration began to break out on her upper lip. He could tease as much as he liked; nothing would induce her to ask for help. Breathing heavily she stopped and looked up. The terrace seemed miles away. Suddenly Pierre dashed past her, leapt up the steps two at a time and leaning against a vast potted plant grinned wickedly down at her. "You look a little tired *ma petite*. No? Well, come on then. Why are you waiting?"

Provoked beyond endurance she flung away the wretched crutches, turned her back on him and sat down. "I refuse to go another inch until you leave me alone!"

"Oh la, la! Now I've made you cross."

His obvious enjoyment of her discomfiture did nothing to appease her annoyance. If he would go away she could push herself up the remaining steps on her backside, but it was out of the question while he was gleefully watching.

"If you come up on your bottom you'll make your dress dirty."

The mind reader again! "I am perfectly capable of climbing a few steps alone," she said frostily.

"Yes, yes I am sure you are," he laughed, and running down the steps he scooped her up in his arms before she had time to object. Breaking into giggles in spite of herself she grabbed wildly at the wisteria trailing along the stone balustrade in a vain attempt to halt him. The long, flower-laden fronds tore away from the serpentine limb of the tree and Pierre walked through the front door garlanded with pale green leaves and exquisite mauve flowers like a Greek god.

Arlene, immaculately groomed, met them in the hall. Her face expressed no surprise at their laughing faces. She cast a sympathetic look at Willow's swollen foot. "Take the poor kid into the study, Pierre. Nicole is preparing her room now."

"Good idea," he agreed. "But she needs watching. She has just tried to strangle me with wisteria!"

Arlene's silvery laugh rang out in the hall. "Bully for you Willow! But don't damage him too much. He is rather important to us all."

The trim figure in the blue linen dress walked in front of them swinging her hips like a model, and calling over her shoulder, "I'm so glad your ankle isn't broken. Your holiday won't be a total write-off."

Willow smiled. Arlene seemed to be a thoroughly nice person.

Pierre put her down on the sofa in the book-lined study. The room was shady and cool and the scent of roses drifted through the open windows.

"Will you be all right here?"

"Yes, thanks. I'll be fine."

"Ring this if you need anything," he said, demonstrating the small silver bell on the table.

"Right, I will."

"Good." He sounded faintly puzzled, as if he were hoping for a different reaction. What exactly? And what could he expect with Arlene looking on? He stretched and smothered a yawn. *"Mon Dieu,* but that was a strenuous night!"

Willow glanced swiftly at Arlene. What a tactless thing to say! What on earth must she be thinking?

The American woman's serene smile did not waver. "I will ask Nicole to bring you a real English breakfast."

Willow shook her head. "No. Please. Really . . ."

"You will east," Pierre said firmly.

Arlene patted her shoulder. "He's right. You must be starving. Eggs, bacon, toast and coffee coming up shortly."

They both went to the door. "I'll look in later to say good-bye," Pierre said.

Willow picked up a magazine. "Yes do," she replied casually.

For a moment he hesitated as if he might return but, apparently thinking better of it, moved on saying, "Arlene, would you kindly ask Jean to pack my valise. Just the gray and blue suits—he will know which ones."

"Only those? You must be going to have a very dull time!" Her laughter trilled away down the

hall and Willow was left in the study marveling at
her self-control. She had not shown the least
dismay when confronted with the guest nestling in
her lover's arms. Either she was a consummate
actress or the bond uniting them was one of rare
understanding.

Jean brought in her breakfast accompanied by
Nicole, his plump, merry faced wife, who was
carrying the despised crutches. "When you're
ready Mademoiselle, Nicole will take you up in
the lift to your room," he said, settling the tray
comfortably across her legs.

"How is Monsieur Anselm today?" she asked.

"Greatly improved we think. Don't we Nicole?"

Nicole giggled and nodded vigorously.

"I believe he is hoping you will feel sufficiently
restored yourself to sit for him this afternoon,"
Jean said.

Willow shook out the linen napkin and spread
it on her lap. "Of course I will."

This time the butler beamed broadly. "Monsieur will be delighted."

At least I have gained the respect of the staff,
Willow thought, plunging a knife into the golden
yolk of an egg.

Her room at the back of the house looked
across the gardens to the mountains. Decorated
in pale green and white, with touches of rose-pink
in the silk curtains and bedspread, it appealed to
both the eye and the senses.

After she had watched the bouncing, red-
cheeked Nicole unpack, Willow maneuvered her-

self outside to the private balcony and sank into a bamboo chaise longue.

A few peaceful, sunshiny days and she would feel as good as new, fully able to return to Number Nine and continue her holiday independently. Until then there was nothing for it but to try to relax and enjoy life.

She was roused from a pleasant doze by voices directly below the balcony.

"You are quite sure?" Pierre's voice.

Arlene's silver laugh. "My darling! Of course I am sure. Anyway the doctor confirmed it yesterday."

"Are you happy?"

"Well . . ." Arlene's laugh took on a resigned note. "The circumstances could certainly be better."

"Yes, it is a little unfortunate just now. Never mind, you are very capable—you will manage beautifully. I will do everything I can to help. When is the great day?"

"December—the third week. It will be a fine Christmas present for your father."

Willow gasped. It could only mean one thing: Arlene was pregnant. How could she sound so serene, so unconcerned?

"He will be enchanted," Pierre agreed. "Are you certain you are content with the present arrangement? If you would like to change your plans I could fix you up with a flight in a matter of days."

Arlene brushed the suggestion aside. "What kind of a start in life would that give the baby? No, I will just have to make the best of things for the moment. Anyway—" her voice brightened, "I'm off to Paris to buy myself a truckload of glamorous maternity clothes. Will you still love me when I have a huge stomach and a penchant for pistachio ice cream?"

Pierre chuckled. *"Chèrie* I salute your common sense and courage. As for loving you—Villa Martine is packed with your willing slaves. Come here and let me kiss you."

"Darling, darling Pierrot. What would I do without you?"

Willow put her hands over her ears. She had heard enough—too much in fact. She had no desire to listen to their love-making. Her cheeks burned with embarrassment. How could she spend even one night under his roof when only a few hours ago in the bedroom of Number Nine . . . The memory of that passionate embrace made her heart skip a beat and the blood sing in her veins. To think she had almost . . . And meanwhile the unsuspecting Arlene was patiently waiting to tell him about the baby! How diabolical of him to suggest that she might care to fly off somewhere and leave him in peace, free from all responsibility. How utterly despicable! Would Anselm really be *"enchanté"* to have a grandchild born on the wrong side of the blanket? Perhaps so. He was an artist, possibly such events were accepted as normal in his world.

Picking up the crutches she limped back into the bedroom, her mind in a turmoil. In heaven's name what ought she to do? If she left now and returned to Colombaia everyone in the villa would want to know why. She could hardly explain that she had overheard a conversation—an extremely intimate conversation—which she found deeply disturbing.

Fortunately Pierre's business trip meant that they would not see each other for several days, and when he returned she would be sure to keep herself, be polite but distant. He would soon get the message. As soon as she could stand on two feet she would leave—portrait or no portrait!

Someone knocked on the door. She braced herself. *"Entrez,"* she called.

It opened and Pierre stood on the threshold dressed in a superbly cut, dark blue suit—every inch the successful executive.

"I must be going now."

She smiled brightly. "Must you? Good-bye then."

He stepped into the room and put down his briefcase. "Is that all? Just good-bye?"

"Well . . ." She glanced down at her bare feet. All her toes were curling under like pink snails trying to hide in their shells. "Good-bye and thank you."

"I see. Good-bye and thank you. It is better than nothing I suppose."

"What else do you want?" She flashed irritably.

He started to move towards her. "Perhaps just to see you happy."

"But I am happy!" The words seemed to stick in her throat.

"I have seen you happier," he said wryly.

The closer he came the more she was tempted

to back away. Dear Lord! Didn't he know what he was doing to her? How could he persist in being so cruel?

She raised her eyes, green-cold and hard, to meet his mocking gaze. "I have never been happier," she said deliberately. "Have a good trip Pierre."

He looked at her quizzically. "Is that an order?"

She gripped the crutches until they dug painfully into her hands. "Consider it one if you wish."

His long lips came together in a thin, bitter line. "Very well, I will." Picking up his case, he left the room and closed the door behind him without giving her a backward glance.

Willow stared at the white unrelenting door. Please let him come back. Oh please!

But he did not return and after a few indecisive moments she lifted the telephone by the bed and placed a call to the only person she could trust to tell her what she ought to do—her Aunt Ruth.

Chapter Six

Anselm was waiting for her in the room Pierre had converted into a studio. It was on the top floor of the villa and ran the entire length of the house having long north-facing windows. All his equipment had been brought from Colombaia and laid out with fastidious attention to detail: jars of clean brushes, palette knives, tubes of paint, oddly shaped tools neatly arranged as though in a surgery. A large easel supporting a fresh canvas stood ready for the portrait.

"My son has made sure that I have everything I need," Anselm said, following her admiring gaze.

"It's wonderful," she agreed, "but I don't suppose it feels like home."

"Home?" The old man glanced out of the windows toward his beloved mountains. "I will never live there again. Pierre is right—it is not suitable. I will be very comfortable here and he won't have to worry about me."

Willow slipped her arm through his. "That is a very sensible and courageous decision."

His eyes filled with tears. "You are an understanding child. Now . . ." He patted her hand briskly. "I must not be a sentimental old fool, and we must get down to work." He led her over to the same cane chair with the high fan-shaped back that he had occupied on her first visit, and took away her crutches. "I want you to sit quite naturally." He walked back to the easel and perched himself on a high stool in front of the canvas. "Are you comfortable?"

"I think so."

The old eyes twinkled. "There's nothing to be nervous about. I am the one who should be nervous but I am very excited. Now, will you please look out of the window and tell me what you see."

Willow turned her head. "The gardener is riding a lawn mower up and down the lawn—"

"Is he wearing a tea-pot on his head?"

"A tea-pot?" She looked around—startled, baffled and amused by the mad question.

"Good! Excellent! That is just the look I want." He chortled with pleasure at the success of his ruse. His picture would show a girl on the brink of womanhood—a confused emotional state hovering between alarm and anticipation. He had caught her just in time. Next year she would undoubtedly have discovered her potent femininity and have developed into a spiritually aware, yet voluptuous woman. It would be a fortunate man who gained her trust and love.

"What are you thinking about?" she asked, catching him staring at her with thoughtful distant eyes.

"I am thinking that unless you keep still we will be here until supper!" he growled.

The afternoon passed companionably. For long periods Anselm worked silently and Willow thought how restful it was having one's portrait painted. Eventually he asked her about the mountain escapade and she admitted ignoring Pierre's advice and consequently getting lost and spraining her ankle. She told him how Pierre had found her and carried her home, dwelling, for the old man's pleasure, on his son's gallantry and fortitude.

"The awful thing is that I will never be able to repay him for everything he did," she said at the end of the story.

Anselm squeezed a blob of white paint onto his palette. "Tenacity, courage and generosity are his natural qualities. They do not require remuneration."

Maybe, she thought, but he is also arrogant, and shows a fine disdain for other people's feelings.

"He is very wrapped up in this new hotel," Anselm continued. "It will be the pride of Italy's tourism when it is finished."

It was the perfect opening for the question she had been longing to ask. "What exactly does he do?"

"Castille and Breton are architects. Philippe is based in Paris and Pierre's office is in Menton."

"Where is the hotel?"

Anselm worked his brush back and forth in the paint. "A kilometer or so the other side of the Italian border. He has gone there today but is flying to Paris tonight." He put down the brush and, standing up, massaged the small of his back with his hands. "I think we will rest for a little while."

Willow looked out of the window. Arlene was strolling across the newly cut lawn. She had changed her dress for a chic navy number and her blonde head shone like silk in the sunlight. Willow's heart was suddenly filled with black hatred. She had never known an emotion so overwhelming or so powerful. It passed in seconds, but she knew it had laid bare her deepest feelings about Pierre's mistress.

"I think we have done enough for today." Anselm said. "You are looking tired. We'll start again in the morning. We have done some useful work."

She forced a smile. "I've enjoyed it."

Anselm handed her the crutches, accompanied her to the lift, and walked thoughtfully back to his studio. She had looked exceptionally pale during the latter part of the sitting; he blamed himself for keeping her too long after her harrowing experience. Tomorrow he would have to be more considerate.

Stepping out of the lift Willow was confronted with Arlene, her arms full of yellow roses. She smiled warmly. "Hi! Feel like helping me with these? I'm hopeless with flowers but I gather you are a whiz."

Willow followed her to the flower-room near the kitchens and together they chose a superb crystal vase. Arlene prepared the stalks and Willow created a charming, natural arrangement.

"It looks so easy when you do it," said Arlene enviously.

Willow smiled. "I should hope so! I work with flowers all the time."

"Even so I ought not to be quite so inept." The American gently stroked a golden flower head with plump, white fingers, her long red nails moving over the fleshy petals like drops of blood and suddenly the humiliating truth flashed through Willow's brain: She was jealous! The word reverberated inside her head; she felt dreadfully sick. The warm pressure of Arlene's arm around her waist steadied her.

"Hey, are you okay?" The pretty, good-natured face radiated concern.

"You look awful! We must get you to bed right away! I was flying to Paris tonight but I think perhaps I had better stay with you."

"No!" Willow heard her own voice sharply refuse the offer. "I mean, it's kind of you but I'll be okay after a good night's sleep."

She allowed herself to be taken up to her room and put to bed. Arlene drew the curtains, shutting out the evening sunlight, and placed a cool hand on the girl's damp forehead.

"You feel feverish. I really think I should stay."

"No. Please . . ." It would be unbearable if she stayed! "I just need sleep. Tomorrow I'll be as fit as a fiddle."

Arlene looked doubtful. "You're sure?"

"Positive."

Glancing at her watch, Arlene said, "Then I'd better throw some things into a bag. I must leave for the airport in half an hour. I'll call you tomorrow. Jean knows the Paris number. Don't hesitate to ring."

Willow smiled gratefully. "Thanks."

"*Au revoir* then. See you sometime next week."

She went out, leaving a trace of musky perfume lingering in the air.

Willow stared up at the ceiling. It was white with a delicate, molded cornice. A fat black spider with angular hairy legs boldly returned the stare. Her Aunt Ruth was terrified of spiders. Throughout the year she pursued them relentlessly with brooms, newspapers, fly swatters—anything that came to hand. Willow was not afraid of harmless things like spiders, but she was petrified of the aching, impossible longing rapidly overwhelming her, shaking her, like an earthquake, to her very foundations.

In a couple of hours Pierre and Arlene would be in Paris. They would probably dine at a fashionable restaurant and return to his apartment in the small hours to while away the night in each other's arms.

How could she bear it? Restlessly she twisted her head from side to side on the pillow, a childhood habit that reasserted itself when she was distressed or seeking the solution to a problem. Well, there was no solution to this particular problem. In the space of three days she had fallen passionately in love with a man who was in love with someone else. Put like that it was a simple fact of life. Simple but complicating.

When she had spoken to Ruthie earlier in the afternoon she had failed to disclose the real nature of her trouble. She had merely recounted the mountain adventure in dramatic detail and told her aunt about the Castilles' generous hospitality. Ruth, after her initial anxiety had been assuaged, had agreed that Willow must keep her promise to the old man. "You sound as though you have fallen on your feet my girl," she said.

But had she? What depths of lonely despair would she plumb while Pierre was away? She closed her eyes and instantly imagined his arms around her again—his warm lips searching her eyes, her temples, her soft mouth. "Oh Pierre!" she whispered brokenly. But only the spider heard, and it scuttled away as though embarrassed to hear more.

After two days the swelling in her ankle had gone down considerably and on the third she was able to limp along with the aid of a walking stick. The mornings were fully occupied by the portrait sittings, but the afternoons and evenings were long and tedious. She did some judicious sunbathing and after a few days her skin had lost its English pallor and acquired a glowing tan.

Every day she half-hoped, half-dreaded hearing Anselm announce Pierre's return. But he hardly mentioned his son or the charming American. Once, when Willow asked whether or not he had painted Arlene he smiled and said, "Of course. You don't think I would let a ripe beauty like Arlene escape my brush do you?"

"She is very attractive," Willow agreed. An expression of tenderness crossed his old face. "She is indeed. We Castilles have always been fortunate in our women."

You too! Willow thought recalling an earlier conversation with Pierre. But the manner in which the two men had spoken contrasted strongly. Pierre's remark had been proudly couched, Anselm's stated with gratitude.

Her mood during the lengthy, sun-kissed days was one of tortured self-castigation. Try as she might she was unable to put the Frenchman out of her mind for a moment. Every room contained heartbreaking reminders of his presence: a study of Roman architecture lying on the study desk, his tweed jacket hanging in the cloakroom, his mail mounting up on a salver in the hall. Unable to settle, she wandered from room to room daring to touch objects he handled daily, marveling at things he took for granted: a picture hung in a certain light to bring out the rich colors, a ceramic jar with a fine lustre, a chair—elegantly carved, a rug—intricately woven. It was almost as though by saturating herself in his ambiance, she hoped to blunt her desire for the man himself. If so, the trick failed. The more she soaked up the atmosphere the more she longed and feared to see him again.

Pierre's lavishly furnished bedroom contained a bed large enough to accommodate a sultan's harem. It was covered with a brown fur spread and piled with flame-colored cushions.

Every afternoon she crept into the room and stretched out on the bed with a thumping heart, a guilty craving for the sight, the sound, the touch of the man who slept there ebbing and flowing through her like the relentless tide of the sea.

"You are getting thinner," Anselm remarked one day, his shrewd, experienced eyes taking note of the deepening hollows under the newly acquired tan.

She had made light of the suggestion, but it was true. By the end of the week her skirts and jeans hung loosely around her waist and the bathroom scales confirmed that she had lost six pounds in as many days.

Daily she debated whether or not to return to Number Nine. The need to remain at the villa ceased when she put aside the crutches but Anselm was so absorbed in the portrait that he had begun to demand her presence at odd hours of the day as well as for the agreed morning session. She decided that if she left it would seriously interrupt the flow of work, and so she stayed, growing thinner and dreaming impossible dreams, while the artist altered and re-altered his picture, the original spirit of which continued to elude his skill. It began to express a mysterious sadness as though the sitter, gazing into the painter's eyes, was unable to come to terms with her own reflection.

Late on Thursday the weather clouded over and the morning brought heavy rain.

"No sunbathing today," Anselm said. "What will you do after lunch?"

"I don't know." Her shoulders drooped despondently.

He scraped the canvas with a palette knife. "Poor Willow! This is a very dull way to spend your holiday."

For politeness' sake she usually denied similar remarks, but today she shrugged it off with a *"c'est la vie!"*

Anselm threw down his knife. *"C'est la vie!* You sound like an old woman. You are ruining my picture with your *c'est la vie!"*

"I'm sorry," she sighed.

He picked up a brush and settled down again but his anxiety about her increased.

By five it had stopped raining and Nicole came into the library carrying a tea tray. "You are losing the roses in your cheeks Mademoiselle," she observed. "You must take a walk in the garden before it starts to rain again."

"Must I? Why?"

It was an uncharacteristically rude reply to a courteous suggestion but Nicole only laughed.

"Mademoiselle is like a bear with a sore head today. *N'est ce pas?* Of course you must exercise to strengthen your ankle. Monsieur would wish it."

A rebellious glint appeared in the young guest's eyes. Would he indeed! In that case she just might never exercise again. She might sit sulking over a cup of tea forever. She might pine away and die right there in the gold and ivory salon with the huge Venetian mirrors and fabulous chandeliers.

Nicole poured out the tea and dropped a slice of lemon into the cup. "Monsieur gave me strict instructions to look after you Mademoiselle. I do not like to see you so lonely in this big house. The garden is a better place for you."

Willow smiled gratefully. "You're right Nicole. I'm sorry if I was rude. Of course I must go outside. I only wish I could walk into town but my ankle is not strong enough."

"Walk into town!" Nicole threw up her hands in horror. *"Mon Dieu,* you will be the death of me! You must stay in the grounds so that we all know where you are." She hurried away shaking her head and muttering.

The garden smelled fresh and damp. Throughout her short stay the grounds proved a constant source of delightful surprises. Imaginatively landscaped, they comprised a series of individual gardens connected by stone-flagged, flower-bordered paths; grassy, hedged walks and vine covered archways. In one she discovered a pool in whose depths shoals of coruscant fish darted hither and thither under yellow and white lilies. Another, hidden behind a tall hedge, was laid out in the form of a sundial, each hour represented by a different herb.

Because of her strained ankle she had only been able to explore the lower part of the garden but this evening an immensely long flight of stone steps, ascending between ornamental trees, lured her to a lavender-bordered terrace far above the house from where she gazed rapturously out on the whole delightful patchwork of pattern and colour below and over the roof of the house to the sea.

At the back of the terrace stood a low building with gothic-style windows and an arched doorway. The door was not locked and a glance around the interior told her at once that she had stumbled on Pierre's drawing office. The high desk and chair, graph paper, pencils and geometric instruments all proclaimed "architect." It was an unremarkable, workmanlike place where a man could get on with the job in hand, and photographs on the walls testified to the hard work and success of Castille and Breton.

Limping over to a chair she sat down. On the utilitarian desk were two framed photographs of a small dark boy with clear, merry eyes. A boy not unlike the young Pierre must have been. He must be very fond of the child to have his photograph in front of him every day while he worked. But if he was fond of children why didn't he marry Arlene and acknowledge his own child? It was an incomprehensible situation.

Arlene again! "It's becoming an obsession!" she said aloud.

"What is?"

Startled, she looked 'round. "I didn't hear you come in."

Pierre was standing in the doorway, incredibly tall, dark and palpably alive.

"What is becoming an obsession?"

The shock of seeing him, of being caught trespassing in his inner sanctum, turned her brain to sawdust.

"I can't remember," she said feebly, her eyes fixed on a button of his blazer.

"No?" The polished shoes took a step forward. "You must have a very short memory."

"Yes." Reaching for her cane she stood up.

"You are thinner," he said.

She cleared her throat trying to find a natural tone of voice. "I expect it's your imagination."

Slowly the shining shoes advanced. "Possibly. My imagination has been working overtime lately."

Before she could reply he seized her roughly, pulled her to him, tilted up her chin and brought his insistent mouth down on her lips with a burning intensity.

Her cane clattered to the ground and she pushed him away with all her strength but he grabbed her again, pinioned her arms and kissed her eyes, nose, lips, neck—his hands avidly caressing her quivering body through the thin silk dress.

It was useless to struggle. Before her resolve to repulse him could crumble she froze, became as stiff, unyielding and unresponsive as a wooden pole. But the more she resisted the more hungrily his probing tongue explored her soft mouth, the more skillfully his hands urged her to catch the flame of his desire. Suddenly the implacability of her opposition seemed to penetrate his ardor and, releasing her, he stepped back breathing quickly.

"I'm sorry," he apologized coldly. "I have never forced myself on a woman. I thought . . . never mind, I was wrong."

Taking off his jacket, he hung it carefully on the

back of a chair, loosened his necktie and calmly slit open a letter.

Willow watched him, her heart pounding with love, resentment and regret, but he continued to work, apparently unmindful of her presence.

Minutes ticked by. The silence was driving her mad. "I have no wish to be added to your list of conquests!" she exclaimed suddenly.

He did not look up. "What list?"

She laughed bitterly. "I am sure you have one. Two probably."

"Mais oui, two of course!" he mocked. "Soon no doubt it will be three!"

He was making her look foolish again.

She bent down to retrieve her cane. "No doubt!

"That's right, make a joke of it!" she burst out, furiously bashing a stool with her cane. "Make a joke of everything—life, love everything—laugh at it all. Nothing can touch you because you're so bloody pleased with yourself!"

The unexpected tirade made him raise his head. "Tut, tut! Words like that are reserved for the grown-ups."

"Are they?" she said between gritted teeth. "Well, perhaps I am growing up at last!"

Putting down the letter Pierre strolled towards her. "I doubt it," he said softly.

Nervously, she backed away. Had she gone too far? He was smiling, but it was a smile without humor and the blue eyes had turned to ice.

"There is no need to look like a scared rabbit," he said contemptuously. "I am not going to attack you again. I like warm, responsive women, not frigid little girls with hang-ups about big bad Frenchmen!"

"So I've noticed!"

A tensing of muscles in his jaw hinted at barely controlled anger. "I see. Well, I have work to do so if you will excuse me . . ." He went back to the desk and again picked up a pencil.

"By all means." She limped quickly through the office and was halfway across the terrace before she heard him call her name. She looked 'round reluctantly. "Yes?"

He came outside, shielding his eyes from the evening sun. "You're walking better now. Does that mean you could manage to do some flowers for the dining room tomorrow? I am giving a dinner party for an important client. Arlene usually does them but she is still in Paris. I would be most grateful for your help."

Willow was dumbfounded. He spoke as calmly as if nothing unusual had passed between them, as if the recent scene had never taken place, as if all that naked passion had never been unleashed.

He was politely waiting for her to reply. There was no special appeal in the cool blue eyes. He would not be disturbed if she refused. Perhaps she had finally succeeded in making him indifferent to her. Well if she had, so much the better.

"How many guests are you having?" she asked coldly.

"Ten. You are included of course."

She shook her head. "I'm afraid not."

"No?" He looked mildly irritated. "Why not?"

"I haven't brought a dinner dress." The best possible excuse!

His face cleared. "Is that all? Then I will see you have something suitable by tomorrow evening."

"Oh I couldn't . . ."

But without waiting to hear why she couldn't he disappeared inside the office and closed the door between them.

Slowly she made her way down the long steps into the cool, shadowy garden. A bird, hidden in a nearby tree warbled merrily, "He's back! He's back! He's back!" And Nicole, passing her on the stairs, twittered, "Is it not good to have Monsieur back, Mademoiselle?" Her round, black eyes were shining with pleasure.

Everyone in the place—except her—seemed to be revitalized by Pierre's return. Why then was her heart full of such dread? Who was she afraid of—him or herself?

Chapter Seven

Grasping the opportunity to repay a fraction of the Castilles' hospitality Willow decided, unasked, to decorate the main staircase and the reception rooms in addition to the dining room.

Anselm agreed to release her from the Saturday "sitting" and she spent the morning touring the garden and glass-houses with Georges, the head gardener.

Jean managed to find vases needed for all the luxuriant, casual arrangements Willow enjoyed creating and with the help of Nicole and her sister, Bette, the work was finished by late afternoon. Every room from the library to the salon was redolent with a flowery fragrance and glowed with color.

Standing in the dining room Willow surveyed her handiwork with pleasure. The Canterbury bells and white roses perfectly complimented the antique silver. The effect was fresh but not cold. She had placed knots of blue and white flowers on each snowy table napkin and a tall stand of agapanthas, delphiniums and lilies behind the host's chair. Not bad, she thought looking around, not bad at all. Thank goodness she had not lost her touch!

"Mademoiselle."

Hearing Jean's voice she turned. "Yes?"

"A gentleman wishes to see you. A Mr. Holder."

Steven! Grabbing her cane she limped quickly out to the hall. There he was: very fair, very healthy and English-looking, casually dressed in his old sports jacket and flannels.

"Steve! What a surprise!"

He advanced, took her in his arms and kissed her firmly on the mouth. "Darling! I hope you are pleased."

"Of course I . . ." She floundered, suddenly unable to utter the assurance he wanted.

But Steve, busy taking in details of the flower-decked hall, failed to notice her hesitation. "Is there somewhere we can talk privately?"

"I suppose so." She took him into the library where he plumped himself down on the red leather sofa.

Willow saw his critical gaze rove over the gold-tooled spines of the books. "I bet this fellow doesn't have to work for his living," he muttered enviously.

"As a matter of fact he does," she said, thinking how ungainly he looked slumped on Pierre's sofa.

He patted the red leather confidently. "Well, come here and tell me you are glad to see me."

She sat down primly, leaving a cushion's width between them. "Of course I am." It did not sound altogether convincing.

"You look a bit of a mess," he said. "What have you been up to?"

Willow glanced down at her creased skirt and stained hands. "Working," she replied shortly.

He registered the vase of crimson and cream roses on the desk without visible appreciation. "Oh yes? Are all those flowers in the hall your doing then?"

"Yes."

He grinned and winked a knowing eye. "I hope you are charging the chap a bomb."

"Certainly not!" she replied sharply. "The Castilles have been very generous to me. Pierre is giving a dinner party tonight. This is the least I can do to thank them."

"Pierre Castille? You mean the fellow you went mountaineering with?"

"We didn't go mountaineering," she explained patiently. "I went off alone and got lost in the mist. Pierre found me and brought me home."

"Ruth said something about your ankle. Is that why you are walking with a cane?"

"It is." How long would this catechism continue?

"And is that why you left the house in the mountains?"

"Of course. After the accident the Castilles kindly invited me to stay here."

Steven frowned. "Who are these Castilles?"

"Pierre and his father Anselm Castille, the artist."

"But why didn't you come back to England? Surely they would have helped you get a flight?"

"Because Anselm was in the middle of painting my portrait and I didn't want to let him down."

Steven grunted sceptically. "There must be dozens of girls in Menton he could paint."

Willow clenched her fists in her lap. At all costs she must not allow him to rile her; he always got the best of it when she lost her temper. "He happened to want to paint me," she said firmly.

Sliding along the leather seat he wrapped a hot, tweedy arm around her waist. "Come along darling," he coaxed. "Relax. You haven't given me a proper kiss yet."

Willow stiffened and tried to draw away then, deliberately, she removed his arm and faced him squarely. "Steve, why exactly have you come?"

He withdrew, assuming a pained expression. "Why have I come? To take you home of course."

"But I am not due to go home yet."

"Oh really Willow!" Exasperated, he flopped back against the red leather.

The interview was turning out to be more difficult than he had anticipated, but he had apparently decided to humor her for a while. "Ruth is worried about you. She said you sounded miserable though I must say you look blooming to me."

"What makes you think I want to come home?"

she asked. "This is my holiday and whatever you may think I am enjoying it."

"Really?" His eyes swiveled to the flowers on the desk. "Working your fingers to the bone for a man who could afford to send for the best florist in Paris? A busman's holiday, I call it. Well anyway . . ." He shrugged off the argument. "The point is you can't stay here, it's not suitable."

"Why?"

He leaned forward and placed a hot, moist hand on her knee. "Because you are engaged to me. Remember?"

She decided that prevarication was the best form of defense. "I don't remember an engagement exactly. We did talk about a possible arrangement in the future."

Steven let out a loud guffaw. "Really? Is that why you kept on at me to make it official? You seemed to think it was a pretty tight arrangement before you left England!"

The barb struck home and she pushed away the possessive hand impatiently. "I still don't see why it is unsuitable for me to stay here."

"Oh for heaven's sake grow up!" He glanced out of the library door to make sure no one was hanging about the hall. "According to Ruth— who got it from Mrs. Bell—this fellow Castille is a bachelor and a pretty unsavory one at that."

"That doesn't sound like Mrs. Bell."

"Willow, the fact is you can't possibly stay under his roof with only his decrepit old father and a few servants."

And his mistress! Willow thought. Aloud she asked "Why not?"

"Because everyone will think you're having an affair with him," he said bluntly.

"Oh, now I see!" She uttered an angry, tinkling laugh. "You don't trust me. Why didn't you say so?"

He ran his hands distractedly through his short tow-colored hair. "It's not you I don't trust, it's him."

"But you don't know him," she pointed out logically.

"I don't need to," he sneered. "Chaps like that are all the same. They think money can buy anything."

"Me for example."

"Yes . . . I mean no, of course, not you!" Getting up, he shoved his hands in his pockets and walked disconsolately over to the book shelves.

Willow felt almost sorry for him. Steven was no good with words; she had always been able to run rings around him in an argument. Generally he took refuge in childish obstinacy until she gave in.

"Anyway, Pierre already has a romantic attachment," she assured him with deceptive cheerfulness.

"Really?" He looked decidedly brighter.

"Yes. So you needn't worry yourself about my virtue!" She turned away to hide the faint color creeping into her cheeks at the lie. If Steve had seen her in Pierre's arms yesterday afternoon, had witnessed the feverish kisses, the impatient seeking hands, he would not be so easily reassured.

"That never stopped a man making a pass at a girl." Steven was looking at her curiously, as if seeing her properly for the first time since his arrival. "What on earth is the matter with you? You are behaving very oddly."

"Yes. I'm sorry." She too was seeing him with fresh eyes: a short, thick-set, red-faced man with moody flaring nostrils and a self-willed mouth. At home, on the farm, she had always thought him so good-looking, and had borne his highhanded, possessive manner patiently, hoping it would change after they were married. Was it seeing him out of context that made him seem so different? Or did it have something to do with a tall Frenchman with a scarred face and a rare, bittersweet smile that made her heart turn over? Of course it did. No point in denying it.

"Men like Pierre Castille are never content with one woman," Steven said. "You are quite attractive, you know."

"Thanks." Something odd must have come over Steve; he never handed out compliments!

He gave her an embarrassed grin. "I haven't arrived empty-handed," he said, putting his hand in his pocket. "Come and see."

She got up and went over to him. "What is it?"

He handed her a small box. "Open it."

The diamond inside winked brightly in its velvet bed. She gazed at it silently thinking, a month ago I would have been overjoyed.

"Well . . . do you like it?"

He was smiling, anticipating her pleasure.

"Of course, but . . ."

"Put it on then. Here—let me." Taking out the

ring he fitted it onto the fourth finger of her left hand. The diamond glittered, then suddenly slipped sideways.

"I knew you'd gotten thinner," he said accusingly.

Willow looked at him steadily. "Why now Steve? Why did you choose this particular moment?"

He snapped the box shut and replaced it in his pocket. "Because I want you to return to England with me tonight as my official fiancée. We can be married the Saturday before Harvest Festival. I've told Mum and Dad and made all the right noises to your father and your aunt. Everyone's delighted and Mum's planning a party for us tomorrow evening."

"I see. So it's all arranged."

He nodded. "Dad has promised to let us have the cottage in the Gulley."

"I see," she said again.

"Well?"

"Well what?"

"You haven't said you are pleased."

She twisted the loose ring 'round and 'round her finger. "What did your parents say when you told them?"

Steven brushed an imaginary speck of dirt off the sleeve of his jacket. "Well er . . . it came as a bit of a surprise of course."

"Did it? After seeing us go out together for over two years?"

"Oh you know parents—they never notice these things."

"Don't they?" The cynical note in her voice was inescapable.

"All right." Moving away he leaned against the book shelves and folded his arms. "Let's have it. What's wrong? What have I done?"

Willow shook her head in amazement. "You really don't know, do you? Then I'll tell you. For two years you obstinately refuse to consider an engagement and now, suddenly, without consulting me, you tell everyone, you set the day and then you expect me to fall over myself with gratitude."

"I expect nothing of the kind . . ."

The red-gold curls bobbed up and down angrily. "I know quite well why you waited so long Steve, you couldn't face your mother. I was always the girl from the cottage—an enthusiastic, extra farm hand. She certainly never envisaged me as a future daughter-in-law! She wanted you to marry a well-bred girl with a rich Daddy. Well, I am not that girl, Steve, so put this ring back in its box, it's too big for me in every respect. I could never fulfill the expectations of the job!"

Steven stood up decisively. "I've had enough of this nonsense. Put on that ring at once and go and pack. Our plane leaves at nine. You are spending the night at the farm and I will take you home in the morning."

"No!"

He gave an incredulous laugh. "What do you mean no? You surely don't expect me to take all that seriously?"

"By no I mean no," she said emphatically. "No

I am not coming with you. No I will not put on the ring. No we are not engaged—if we ever were— and no I will not marry you but thanks for the offer."

He stepped forward, squaring his shoulders for the final battle. "I am a patient man but you are being extremely difficult. Now stop behaving like a spoilt kid and get a move on."

She held out the ring. "Better take it Steve. Perhaps it will fit the next girl."

A deep, offended red suffused his face. Striking the ring from her hand he seized her shoulder and began to shove her towards the door.

Raising her cane she brought it down brutally on his arm. "Leave me alone!"

He fell back, rubbing a bruised wrist. "What on earth has got into you? You have changed beyond recognition."

She had. A few days ago she would no more have struck Steve than have jumped off a cliff.

"I'm sorry," she said contritely. "I hope I didn't hurt you."

Steven pulled up his sleeve, revealing an ugly red weal. "I should jolly well say you did."

"Then you shouldn't have provoked me."

"Provoke you?" He uttered a hollow laugh. "You give a girl a ring—she throws it back at you and whacks you with a cane into the bargain. Some provocation!"

"You pushed me," she pointed out quietly.

"Yes, I'm sorry about that." He looked at his watch. "Look we haven't got much time left. Run off and pack, there's a good girl."

"No Steve," she said patiently, "I'm not going with you." She placed a conciliatory hand on his arm. "Thank you for asking me to marry you but I just can't do it. You shouldn't have taken it for granted."

He shook his head, nonplused by her continued resistance. "But we have always taken it for granted. Both of us. We knew we would marry one day. Everyone knew."

Willow smiled sadly. "Your parents didn't."

"Oh them!" He dismissed his mother and father with an airy wave of the hand. "They'll soon get used to the idea. Anyway they both had to admit that you would make the perfect farmer's wife."

"I would have, a week ago," she said thoughtfully. "But not now."

A look of genuine bewilderment clouded the gray eyes. "But why? I don't understand."

Willow took his hand. How could she explain without hurting him even more? "Because it wouldn't work," she said compassionately.

"But I always thought you loved me," he muttered.

She nodded. "So did I. But I was wrong. I am sorry."

He stared at her for a long moment, searching her face for hopeful signs. "You'll change your mind."

"No."

"What shall I tell them at home?"

"You'll think of something," she said encouragingly.

Now that it was over she wanted to comfort him. She had never seen him so deflated, so unsure of himself.

"May I congratulate you on the flowers, Willow. The house looks magnificent."

The familiar voice sent shivers up her spine. How much had he heard standing out there in the hall? "Thank you," she said breathlessly. "I am glad you think they are all right."

"All right? You English pride yourselves on your understatement. Good evening. I am Pierre Castille." He advanced towards Steven, hand outstretched.

Willow hovered between them. "Pierre, this is Steven my . . . friend from England."

The men shook hands. "Are you staying long in Menton?" Pierre inquired politely.

"Perhaps. I have booked at the Grande." He turned to Willow. "You know where to reach me if you should change your mind."

I won't, she thought. When you leave here it is *adieu* Steven. *Adieu* to a safe future among the fields, woods and hollows of my childhood, *adieu* to the false dream I cherished for so long.

"Give my love to Dad and Ruth," she said. "Tell them I am O.K."

As they walked through the cool flowery hall Pierre offered to have Steven driven to the hotel by his chauffeur. He accepted and kissed Willow's cheek.

Her eyes filled with tears. "Goodbye Steve. Take care."

She watched them go down the steps to the waiting car: the short, heavily built young man with the downcast expression and sun-bleached hair, and the tall, loose-limbed Frenchman for the love of whom she had just destroyed her whole future.

Chapter Eight

The dress had completely slipped her mind until she saw it in the bedroom—black, short and simple—drooping limply from its hanger. Pierre had been as good as his word. She glanced at it without enthusiasm. It looked rather dull and she had never worn black but it was probably more suitable than anything she had brought to France. Fortunately it would go with her new strapy sandals. Anyway she was only going to the dinner out of politeness so what did it matter how she looked?

From her window the purple mountains, remote and exciting, beckoned her back to Colombaia with long shadowy fingers. If only she had been going to dine with Pierre on the candlelit terrace of Number Nine . . . Instantly she

checked the thought. It was crazy to allow herself
to daydream like that. Pierre and Arlene belonged together, now more than ever.

Limping over to the dressing table Willow
picked up her hairbrush but the wild reflection in
the mirror stayed her hand in midair. She looked
as though she had crawled through a flowering
hedge backwards. Her red-gold hair was sprinkled with leaves and petals—her face dirty, her
nose yellow with pollen, her clothes and hands
stained green. . . . ! It would take ages to repair
the damage; a rest was out of the question.

Hastily she washed her hair and allowed it to
dry naturally in the sun while she buffed her
work-worn nails to a pearly shine with Ruth's old
fashioned chamois buffer. A suggestion of frosted
eye shadow and a touch of browny-pink lipstick
completed her make-up. She spent far too long
attempting to create a sophisticated hair style, but
the springy tendrils obstinately defied clips and
combs and insisted on framing her face in their
usual careless manner.

Pulling the dress off its hanger she slipped it
over her head. With a faint sigh the pure silk
jersey settled on her body like a second skin
leaving her shoulders nearly bare. Willow turned
to look at herself in the long mirror. The long
narrow sleeves stressed the grace of her arms, the
exquisitely cut bodice molded perfectly to her
figure and the skirt flowed, light and free as air,
around her legs. It might have been made for her.
Unfortunately the white straps of her bra failed to
enhance the total effect and, quickly undoing the

zip, she removed the offending garment. The dress label embroidered with the word Inigo caught her eye. She stared. Inigo: one of the most famous couturiers in the world! The dress must have cost hundreds of pounds. Had generosity or pride prompted Pierre to choose it in preference to the thousand modestly priced dresses he could have bought instead? Pride, she decided, doing up the zip again; he would not want his friends to think she was a penniless nobody from England.

She groped in the dressing table drawer for the gold bracelet Ruthie had given her for her twenty-first birthday but it was not there. Vainly she scrabbled among her handkerchiefs and scarves. Where on earth could it be? She remembered wearing it on Thursday because Anselm had admired it but could not recall taking it off when she went to bed. Never mind—there was no time to look for it now.

She picked up her cane, then on impulse hung it on the back of a chair. If she could manage without it no one would ask awkward questions about the silly accident.

A quick spray of perfume and a final glance in the mirror. Pierre had chosen well. The black dress offset her suntanned shoulders, slender neck and delicately poised head with its bright halo of hair. The soft material clung to her breasts revealing their firm contours.

All right, she thought—here goes! Holding her head high she walked to the door and opened it. The hubbub of arriving guests floated up to the landing.

"Pierre darling! Gorgeous to see you again!"

"Has Carlo arrived yet?"

"Anyone seen Carlo?"

"The ruffian's probably still at the bottle!"

"My friend! Still living in the same old slum then?"

"We passed the Princess on the autoroute. My dear, I swear the old thing was asleep behind the wheel!"

Steeling herself for the coming ordeal Willow walked to the head of the stairs. Pierre and a guest were conversing in the hall. Although he could not have heard her Pierre suddenly looked up, flooding her with his blue gaze, his face unsmiling, his expression strangely intent. The two men watched in silence as she slowly descended the stairs.

Afraid to meet Pierre's eyes in case he could somehow see straight into her thundering heart Willow fixed her gaze on the stranger. A heavily built man of medium height with iron grey hair, wearing a dark suit and tinted spectacles.

"Bruno this is Willow Hale from England. Willow, this is Bruno Ventura. He has been admiring your flowers."

The stranger took her extended hand, kissed it lightly, held it briefly and relinquished it with distinct but decorous reluctance.

"Pierre, you didn't tell me that I had not yet seen the most exquisite flower of all," he said in a deep, velvety voice with a strong Italian accent.

"Thank you Signore. I hope you are not too free with such compliments," laughed Willow, speaking Italian. "We English are inclined to believe what we hear."

The eyes behind the tinted glasses flashed humorously. "I promise I have not handed out that particular one today." He turned to Pierre. "She is not only beautiful but speaks Italian as well! This will be an evening to remember."

"Yes, Willow has many talents," Pierre said casually. His expression did not change but she hoped the other man had not detected the mocking gleam in his host's eyes.

"Indeed? Then I shall be charmed to learn more about them." He held out his hand. "Come Signorina, allow an old man the privilege of stealing you away from the young bloods for a while. We will drink each other's health and you will explain how you managed to create a flower garden inside Villa Martine."

His hand, large, warm and reassuring closed over hers. "You will excuse us, my friend?"

Pierre inclined his head. "Of course. But first I must compliment Willow on her dress."

She nodded coolly, her emotions in a turmoil under his searching appraisal. "I am glad you approve. I rather like it too."

"Good." Flashing her one of his rare smiles he strolled away to join his other guests.

Bruno Ventura handed her a narrow fluted glass from a tray being carried through the hall.

"Champagne—good champagne—is the prince of wines, best enjoyed before a good lunch but acceptable at almost any time of day. It should never be wasted on undiscriminating palates. If I had my way only the happy pair would be licensed to drink champagne at a wedding. The guests should be offered a lively but unimportant wine to wash down all that disgusting food."

Willow laughed. "If you could make that one stick you would be the toast of parents all over England." She was going to enjoy this man's company; he was amusing and obviously intelligent. It was difficult to tell his age—forty-five perhaps.

"Is your wife with you this evening?" she asked.

"Unfortunately no. I have left her in Milan looking after the family. Pierre may have told you about the hotel we are building across the border —it means of course that I have to spend much of my time here at the moment. My poor wife has learned to bear it."

"It sounds exciting."

"It is," he agreed. "I will tell you all about it at dinner. I believe we are sitting together."

The other guests gathering in the salon were a diverse collection of Europeans. The women well-dressed and self-confident—the men sleek, successful and, Willow thought, amazingly loquacious. One woman, a thin brunette with a long nose, turned to her and rattled off something incomprehensible in French. Seeing Willow hesitate Bruno immediately said, "Mademoiselle Hale is English but she speaks excellent Italian."

The woman stared at her rudely, shrugged and turned to her husband. "*Encore du champagne*," she demanded, waving her empty glass under his nose. They moved away and Willow glanced uncertainly at Bruno.

Bruno shrugged and, drawing her arm through his he said, "Let's ignore that woman, shall we? I would like you to tell me how you built that fantastic edifice in the vestibule. Let's go and look at it."

Leaving the crowded salon they walked arm in arm to the vestibule. At first, unable to believe that he was really interested in her work, she was prepared to point out a few significant details and pass on to the next display. But Bruno, refusing to be hurried, lingered over every arrangement firing questions at her in rapid Italian. How did she choose the colors for each room? What equipment did she use? How long had she trained? Where? How many staff did she employ? What was her turnover and the potential for expansion? He spoke in a low courteous voice sometimes accompanied by a slight smile which seemed to say, I am a bit of a fool about these things, but Willow was not deceived. As they passed from room to room she gradually warmed to his interest and told him more about herself.

He drew it from her naturally and effortlessly, listening attentively to her answers and popping another question whenever she stopped talking. Once, when he removed his glasses to polish them on a monogrammed handkerchief, she glimpsed dark gray eyes under heavy hooded lids and was momentarily—and disconcertingly—reminded of a snake. But he replaced them and the impression passed, leaving a charming man whose obvious wealth and influential position had not eroded his

natural concern for other people or his genuine
interest in their more mundane lives.

After his earlier remark Willow was surprised
to find that they were not sitting next to each
other at dinner. She was placed between an
elderly bearded Frenchman and a fat, bald
German. As they sat down Bruno gave her a
rueful smile from the other end of the table.

Pierre, at the head of the table, had a smartly
dressed gray-haired woman on his right and an
exquisite, fragile blonde on his left. As he opened
out his table napkin he caught Willow's eye and
gave her a sardonic smile. Apparently he was
pleased about something, busy congratulating
himself on some tricky manoeuvre or other. It
couldn't be . . . She glanced at Bruno. He, too,
was looking at Pierre. For a moment the two men
held each other's gaze, then each focused his
attention on his neighbor, and Willow turned to
hers.

The elderly Frenchman, she discovered, was a
retired Professor of Anthropology, who made her
laugh with reminiscences of academic life.

The bulky German on her left spoke no English
and after peering down her cleavage soon gave
the food and wine the full benefit of his attention.

Once Bruno raised his glass to her across the
table and she responded with a quick shy smile.
The Professor noticed. "I see you have another
admirer," he teased. "I think I am a little jealous."

Willow blushed. "I don't think I would call him
an admirer."

"No? I would," he said tersely.

His tone surprised her. "Don't you like him?"

Her companion dabbed his mouth delicately with his napkin before replying. "I don't know him. I know of him of course. Who hasn't heard of Bruno Ventura and his empire—his hotels, yachts and race horses?"

"I haven't, for one," she admitted.

He smiled kindly but refused to be drawn any further on the subject and continued to delight her with his own brand of wit and wisdom until it was time to leave the table.

They were walking towards the salon together when Pierre, excusing himself to the Professor, drew her aside.

"The backgammon tables are up," he said quietly, "but I don't want you to play."

"Why on earth not?" She had always enjoyed playing backgammon at home.

"Because they are a lot of sharks. You would be beaten."

"I don't mind," She laughed.

"They play for money," he said curtly. "A great deal of money."

"We are playing tonight because Bruno enjoys a game. The stakes will be very high."

"Is Bruno the important business connection you told me about?"

Pierre lowered his voice. "Yes. He put up the capital for the new hotel. He has great charisma, is quite ruthless, and has a large yacht and a girl in every port. So be warned."

"Is that why you didn't place us together at dinner?" she asked mischieviously.

He leaned back against the wall and looking down, smiled insolently, his eyes traveling lazily over her from under drooping lids. "No, as a matter of fact. Herr Munchen is an important client too and I knew he would enjoy your company too!"

Willow glared at him, acutely discomforted by Pierre's frankly sexual look. "I shall probably play a game of solitaire, and then go to bed," she said icily.

He nodded. "Good idea. The cards are in the bottom drawer of the desk—Oh, and by the way, I think this is yours."

Putting his hand in the pocket of his beige linen jacket he pulled out her bracelet and dangled it in front of her.

"Thank heavens!" she cried, taking it from him. "Where did you find it?"

Before he could reply a discreet voice from behind him said apologetically, "Monsieur Pierre could you come please. There is a little trouble at one of the tables."

Pierre nodded. "Of course, right away." Willow heard the manservant's retreating footsteps.

"Where did you find it?" she repeated.

Leaning forward he brushed her mouth lingeringly with his, his tongue flickering softly between his parted lips.

"You taste extraordinarily sweet," he murmured. "As for the bracelet . . ." He uttered a quiet laugh. "If you really want to know, it was under my pillow."

"Under your . . . ?" But before she could recover her composure he strode away across the hall, still laughing, to attend to the problem in the salon.

Her mortification complete, she went straight into the study, closed the door and sat down in the big chair behind the desk. So he had found her bracelet under his pillow! She squirmed with embarrassment. It must have dropped off one afternoon when she had been lying on his bed imagining the ecstacy of his unrestrained love-making. He must have discovered it on Thursday night, but decided to give it to her at the party in order to humiliate her. If that was the case he had succeeded brilliantly.

"Am I disturbing you?" The soft Italian voice broke into her thoughts. She sat up with a start, brushing the damp hair back from her rosy face.

"N-no. I thought you were playing backgammon."

Bruno closed the study door, moved noiselessly across the floor and seated himself in the chair facing the desk. "I can play backgammon anytime, but I have only one evening to get to know you."

Willow sat back in the chair unaware of the effect of her creamy shoulders, flushed face and moist young lips on the man before her. "But Pierre has arranged the game 'specially for you."

The Italian puffed at his cigar and waved the smoke away. "Never mind. The others will enjoy it. Anyway as we were not permitted to sit together at dinner there is much I have to say to you."

She smiled ruefully. "I'm afraid I did most of the talking earlier."

He settled his elbows comfortably on the arms of his chair as if preparing for a long stay. "That is what I intended. Tell me Willow, what do you plan to do when you return to England?"

She laughed. "There's not much doubt about that. I shall go back to my job."

"As manageress of this company Florifair?"

She made a small explosive sound of amusement. "Good heavens no! Only of the Brighton branch. But how clever of you to remember the name."

The smoky glasses glinted in the lamplight. "I forget nothing. It is one of the reasons I am where I am today."

Yes, she thought, that is patently true. Ruthless, Pierre had said.

The man in the chair smiled gently, as if to counteract her thought, his full dark lips parting to reveal two rows of large white teeth. "Would it be impertinent of me to ask if you have a boyfriend—someone you hope to marry one day?"

Willow dropped her gaze. "No." Poor Steve, perhaps he was drowning his sorrows in the local wine at this very moment!

"Good." Leaning back his head he gazed thoughtfully at the ceiling. "And I understood you to say that, unfortunately, your mother died some time ago and your father lives with his sister."

"Yes."

"So it comes to this: you have no real ties in England. No one who really depends on you?"

"Well—I do contribute to the support of my father," she admitted shyly. "He is ill and, as far as I know, still out of work."

Bruno waved his cigar airily. "That is merely money."

"Merely money is extremely important to people who haven't any!" she said with asperity.

He reached across the desk for an ashtray exposing a large gold cuff link set with rubies.

"I meant money is merely a commodity. Easily obtainable if you have the correct knowledge and bargaining power."

"But I haven't."

"Maybe not but I have and it was a knowledge and power painfully acquired. Do you think I have always been a wealthy man? That I inherited vast sums and large estates from some fat northern industrialist?"

"I-I don't know," She faltered.

"I grew up in the slums of Naples," he said soberly. "English slums pale in comparison. In the beautiful, the romantic, the ancient city of Napoli it is difficult for the working-class boy to get a job after he is ten."

"Ten!" The green eyes widened in horror.

"Ten," he repeated somberly. "So you see I know all there is to know about poverty."

"I-I'm sorry. I didn't understand."

He tapped the ash from his cigar. "Why should you? Anyway that is not what I wanted to talk to you about. No. I have a proposition to make."

"A proposition?" Willow shifted uneasily.

The powerful shoulders shook with silent laughter. "A business proposition. Purely business."

She smiled with relief. "Oh, I see."

"I have a daughter of about your age," he said, "and a very attractive wife."

Willow colored. A girl in every port Pierre had said. Naturally, she had thought . . ."I'm sorry," she mumbled.

He waved the apology aside. "Think nothing of it. Now tell me how you would feel about running your own shop?"

She gave a puzzled laugh. "Naturally I would be very happy. Why?"

"Because I think you are ready. I questioned you carefully before dinner and listened closely to your answers." Drawing on his cigar he exhaled a perfect smoke ring and watched it dissolve while he was speaking. "You hold a responsible position in your company for one so young and you have talent and skill combined with an infectious enthusiasm for the job. Also—and very important as you will soon see—you speak passable Italian. I imagine that your family encouraged you to keep it up after your mother died?"

She nodded.

"I thought so." He stopped speaking. The silence lengthened. Willow gripped her hands together in her lap. What did he mean? Why didn't he get on with it? But she knew nothing would hurry him. He was a man who knew exactly what he wanted and planned how to get it down to the last detail.

"So," he said at last, "I am going to offer you

your own premises within the shopping complex of my new hotel."

Willow gaped with astonishment. "You mean the hotel Pierre has designed?"

"Castille and Breton have designed it, yes."

"Why me?" The obvious question.

"Why not?" The obvious answer.

"But you must know lots of experienced people who would take it on."

"Of course I do," he said impatiently, "but I happen to think you are the right person. I have had an opportunity to see your work at first hand—your portfolio one might almost say—and after dinner I made a telephone call to a friend of mine in England."

She eyed him warily. "You mean you checked up on me?"

He nodded. "Naturally. Wouldn't you expect me to?"

"I suppose so," she agreed reluctantly.

"Of course. We are both business people. We know that checking is necessary. Everything I learned was to your advantage. Well, how do you feel about it?"

Willow shook her head disbelievingly. "I am overwhelmed. I just don't know what to say."

He smiled. "Then I will say it for you. Thank you for the offer Bruno but I cannot give you an answer until I have seen the place and know what I am taking on."

She bounced excitedly up and down on the springy chair. "Right. When can I see it?"

He shot his wrist out of his sleeve and consulted

a wafer-thin gold watch. "In about an hour if you don't take too long to get ready."

"An hour? You mean tonight?"

He chuckled. "Of course tonight. It is only a few kilometers across the border you know."

She frowned doubtfully. "Wouldn't tomorrow be better?"

"It would," he agreed, "but unfortunately I have to return to Milan as I have an important meeting early in the morning. Of course . . ." He pulled down his cuff down again neatly. "If you would prefer to forget the whole thing. . . ."

"No!" Willow's mind was racing ahead. A flower shop of her own in a luxury hotel on the Italian coast. It was too good an opportunity to let slip through her fingers. "Shouldn't we to wait until the party breaks up?" she asked.

He appeared to consider the suggestion carefully. "No, I don't think so. No one will leave for hours yet and if we get a move on we can be there soon after midnight. I'll show you around and bring you back in time to say good-bye to the delightful old man who fell in love with you at dinner."

Willow jumped to her feet. "I must find Pierre and tell him we are going."

Bruno stubbed out his cigar and stood up. "I wouldn't if I were you."

"Why not?"

Casually he brushed a speck of ash off the lapel of his suit. "Because the last time I saw him he was *tête-a-tête* with the lovely blonde placed—not by accident I imagine—next to him at dinner."

"Oh." The light died out of her eyes and the lively expression faded from her face. "In that case I'll go up and fetch my coat," she said quietly.

"Good." He walked to the door. "I will wait for you in the vestibule. Shall we say five minutes? Don't forget your passport." He held the door open for her and, without casting a look in the direction of the noisy salon, she went straight upstairs to her room.

Nicole was turning down the bed. She looked up as Willow came in. "Is Mademoiselle retiring already?"

"Good heavens no! I've just . . ." She hesitated; it might be wise not to mention the expedition to Nicole, after all, it was not very polite of her to run out on the party, even if only for an hour or two. ". . . come up to get something," she finished.

Nicole punched the pillows energetically. "Isn't it a splendid party, Mademoiselle?

"And Madame Victorine—does she not look superb?"

"Madame Victorine—who is she?"

"The lady with the blonde hair and the fine figure."

"Oh her." Willow shrugged. If Pierre wanted to amuse himself with Victorine it was none of her business.

Nicole carefully draped the silk bedspread over a chair and headed for the door. "Good night Mademoiselle."

"Good night Nicole." When she had gone Willow opened the cupboard and took down her velvet jacket. Throwing it over her arm she left the room and walked quickly downstairs.

Reaching the open salon she paused and looked inside. The backgammon tables were all occupied. Pierre and the blonde woman were seated at one, their heads bent in rapt concentration. As she watched, Victorine placed a hand on her host's shoulder, and whispered something in his ear. He laughed, took the hand and lightly kissed the palm.

With a rapidly beating heart Willow walked past them into the jasmine-scented vestibule. Bruno was waiting outside on the terrace.

"I'm sorry I'm late," she said breathlessly.

He shrugged. "We have plenty of time."

When they reached the top of the steps he took her arm. "Allow me. I expect your ankle is still rather weak. We don't want any more accidents."

His arm felt comforting, and she was glad of its steadying support. Vaguely she wondered who had told him about the accident but then remembered he had already shown himself capable of finding out anything about her. Anything at all. It was a little unnerving.

She looked up at the full creamy moon shining against a star-studded backdrop of soft, deep blue. The wisteria entwining the balustrade glimmered, pale as milk, as they went down the stone steps. The roses nodded peacefully in the well-tended beds. From the house the sound of music and laughter overflowed into the garden, and before them the illuminated town threw a nimbus of light far into the sky.

A long black car was waiting by the steps.

Bruno opened the door to allow her to get in, then let himself into the driver's seat, removed his glasses and slipped them into his pocket.

"*Andiamo*. Let's go."

The engine purred into life and the car glided quietly away from the house, down the avenue of trees and out of the great iron gates.

"Are you comfortable?" he asked.

"Yes thank you."

"Then if you will permit an old man to indulge in a little nostalgia we will have some music." Reaching out he pressed a loaded cassette into position.

A superb tenor voice filled the car: a passionate, throbbing voice lamenting the beauty and poverty of Naples, the cruelty of unrequited love.

After the haunting music had died away Willow looked at Bruno and was deeply touched to see a large tear slowly trickling down his cheek. Tentatively she laid a sympathetic hand on his arm.

He patted it. "Let's hear the other side," he said gruffly and turned the tape over.

Chapter Nine

After a brief holdup at the border they were soon on their way again, cruising smoothly through the balmy night.

"I suppose you think I am a sentimental buffoon," Bruno remarked when the lilting Neopolitan songs ended.

"I think it's nice that you are so deeply attached to your native city," Willow said.

He uttered a harsh laugh. "Attached? I hate the place. The trouble is I can't escape it. Napoli is in my system—I will never be free. One of my companies is based there."

"That must give you pleasure."

"Not pleasure, satisfaction. It gives me a great deal of satisfaction."

A strange reply. She had never thought about the difference between pleasure and satisfaction before. A long gallop across the South Downs gave her both. On the other hand her job was more satisfying than pleasurable. But Pierre's kisses; the tantalizing touch of his hands on her flesh; the banked fire in his blue eyes, capable of burning away her clothes across the length of a dining table, leaving her trembling and confused —these things gave her incredible pleasure but no satisfaction at all. They merely made her hunger for deeper kisses. How long could she hold her own emotions at bay? The next time he kissed her would she be able to stop herself from responding to his forceful masculinity, her hands from exploring his hard body, her lips from caressing the darkly fringed lids of those smoldering eyes?

Deliberately emptying her mind of disturbing thoughts she sat back and tried to enjoy the journey. The car, moving at a leisurely pace, kept plunging into mysterious lakes of shadow cast by buildings, trees and the rocky contours of the coast road, only to re-emerge into the moonlight and bear them quietly along by the sea, glossy as oiled silk under the star-strewn sky.

Suddenly Bruno said, "We will go now, eh?" and the car leapt forward like a famished tiger after its prey. Clinging to her seat Willow riveted her gaze to the speedometer: a hundred; a hundred and twenty; a hundred and sixty; two hundred kilometers per hour. A mighty wind rushed through the car whipping her hair about her face; the squealing of hot tires rent the air as they hurtled 'round corners. Dragging her eyes away from the quivering needle she caught glimpses of flying houses, street lights, road signs. Trees seemed to spring back in terror and the very sky ahead seemed to split asunder as they ripped through sleeping villages.

"Are you enjoying the ride?" Bruno asked, his compact body shaking with laughter.

She plucked nervously at her safety belt. "We seem to be going rather fast!"

"You haven't seen anything yet!" he promised and, good as his word, accelerated the superbly built machine to the limits of its capability.

We will have an accident, Willow thought, watching the needle rise higher and higher. We will go out of control and hit something; both of us will be mangled in the wreckage. Steve will have to break the news to Dad and Ruthie; Anselm will never finish his portrait. What do I regret leaving, she asked herself, certain that the car would crash. One thing. Only one. I will never see Pierre again, never hear his voice, never touch him as I long to do. Then she felt the car swoop round a bend, speed up a long curving hill, bank sharply and begin to descend again, mercifully slowing down to a more reasonable speed. It began to look as if they might escape death after all. She looked at Bruno. His fleshy face radiated excitement, his eyes under the heavy lids shone with pure pleasure.

"That was some ride, eh?"

Willow drew a deep breath. "I don't like driving so fast," she said quietly.

Immediately the triumphant look on his face slipped into an expression of deep concern. "I am so sorry. How thoughtless of me. Of course it must have been very frightening for you. Driving fast cars is one of my personal indulgences. One is inclined to forget other people are not used to it. Please forgive an old man."

If only he wouldn't keep harping on his age, she thought! Especially as he was not particularly old. Nothing like as old as Anselm or the charming professor she'd met at dinner. "I forgive you," she said lightly. "Now let's see what we've come to see."

Bruno parked the car behind some trees and they walked under the sighing branches to the open driveway in front of the hotel. The long white building, backed by the dark hillside, testified proudly to the imaginative work of Castille and Breton. The design was simple, yet pleasing; it was a series of small buildings rather than one large unit. Its calm, cloistered appearance, more reminiscent of a monastery than a hotel, gave the impression of peace and privacy within. Willow liked it immediately. She turned, smiling, to the Italian.

"It's lovely."

"It will be when it's finished." Taking her arm Bruno led her across to the low retaining wall bordering the drive. Far below them the sea, dashing against the rocks on the private beach, sent up showers of sparkling spray.

"We have three swimming pools," he said, pointing them out with a stubby finger.

"Very impressive," Willow agreed. "And you seem to have done most of the landscaping already."

"The hotel is built on the grounds of an old villa," Bruno told her. "The house itself was beyond repair but we have gone a long way toward restoring the gardens. We have even rebuilt and restocked the aviary."

"The aviary? Why?"

"I like birds," he replied blandly. "They are colorful, gay and amusing. Now . . ." taking her arm he propelled her towards the hotel entrance. "We will open a bottle of champagne and drink to the success of your future at the Paradiso."

"Is that the name of the hotel?"

"Can you think of a better one?"

Willow glanced over her shoulder at the luxuriantly flowering beds and avenues of palm trees. It might indeed turn out to be paradise for her. "No, I can't," she admitted. "When can we see the shop?"

He patted her hand. "It won't run away you know. First I must show you the lounges, dining rooms, kitchens and so on—unless of course you are not interested."

"Of course I am," she declared stoutly. It was rather late to tramp 'round an entire hotel but she must at all costs appear enthusiastic.

The glass entrance doors slid silently open before them and a man wearing the uniform of a security guard stepped forward, a leashed Alsatian dog at his side.

"Ah Signore it is you," he said, in rapid Italian. "Pepe here had noticed something."

Bruno bent down to pat the dog. "You didn't look properly. Pepe knows me don't you old fellow?"

The dog wagged its heavy black tail appreciatively.

Carl looked nervously at his employer's bent head. "Yes, Pepe knows," he agreed jocularly.

"We are going to have a look 'round and then we will go up to the penthouse," Bruno said. "Tell Claudio, will you? I don't want to be disturbed."

"Certainly Signore." The guard tugged the dog's lead and together they disappeared into the office behind the reception area.

"When is all the furniture arriving?" asked Willow as they clopped noisily across the empty foyer.

Bruno shrugged. "When the builders have finished. There have been a few last minute problems."

"Nothing serious, I hope."

He tucked a—by now familiar—hand into the crook of her elbow. "Nothing you need worry your pretty, intelligent head about."

They covered miles of bare concrete; looked at three lounges, all with long windows facing the sea; two restaurants, one of them with a marble terrace where the guests would dine and dance under the stars; an indoor swimming pool— empty of water; conference rooms, cloakrooms, bedrooms and finally the kitchens.

"Well," Bruno said, finally coming to rest on the edge of a steel counter. "What do you think of the Paradiso?"

Willow racked her brain for suitable adjectives to bestow on his absorbing new project. "It is going to be marvelous," she said carefully. "Of course it is a little difficult to imagine what the final effect will be when the carpets and furniture are in place. By the way where is the shopping complex?"

Bruno extracted a cigar from a leather case and clipped the end with a tiny gold clipper. "I told you not to be in such a hurry. First I want you to see the penthouse."

"The penthouse?" she echoed in dismay. "Have we time?"

He looked at his watch. "Plenty. It's not yet one."

She wrinkled her forehead doubtfully. "I think we ought to be back by two."

"So do I," he agreed, lighting his cigar. "So let's go."

Sighing inwardly she obediently followed the stocky, energetic figure along the corridor to the lift. She was far from sure that she wanted to be alone with Bruno in the penthouse but in a sense she was on trial. Her future at the Paradiso could well depend on her ability to handle this unusual man sensibly. With any luck it would all be over in a few minutes and they would be on their way back to Menton.

"We are lucky the lift is working," Bruno remarked as the doors closed. "Otherwise it would have been a long walk."

It certainly would, she thought grimly, watching the floor numbers tick by in the lighted panel.

To her amazement when the lift doors opened they stepped into a small, luxuriously carpeted anteroom furnished with expensive modern furniture.

"What a difference!" she remarked with genuine admiration.

"Yes." Bruno ushered her through white double doors into the sitting room. "You are now in the Executive Suite where all the real work is done." He led her through into a large office. "And in here we try to cure all the troubles in Paradise!" he joked.

Yes, she thought, playing God again!

"Through there you will find the bedroom and through that the bathroom." he said pointing to a door leading off the main room. "Perhaps you would like to leave your jacket in the bedroom while I open a bottle of wine."

The bedroom, decorated entirely in creamy beige from the large, low bed to the hessian-type curtains hanging at the wide windows, was restful and uncluttered. Taking off her jacket she put it on the bed. If only he would get on with it they could see the shop, discuss the financing and return to Menton in time to wave off the last guests. But she must go very carefully, she would need his support and good will every step of the way. What would Dad and Ruthie say when they knew she would be running her own shop at the Paradiso? They would be so excited, so proud. Of course they would be sad to see her leave England but she would probably make enough money to pay for them to come out and stay with her.

Willow hugged herself in anticipation. She must remember to send Mrs. Bell a large bunch of flowers when she arrived back in Brighton, a thank you present for introducing her to Colombaia and the most thrilling two weeks of her life.

When she returned to the sitting room Bruno

was standing outside on the roof garden, jacket-less, his gray head silvered with moonlight.

"Ah there you are." He beckoned her with his cigar.

"This must be a very pleasant way to spend one's working life," she remarked, joining him in front of a table set with a champagne bottle, two glasses and a bowl of fresh fruit.

Stripping the wire off the bottleneck, he asked, "What shall we call your business?"

"Something simple," she said, sitting on the swing seat.

He passed her a full glass. "Flowers of Paradise?"

"No, no!" she laughed. "That's far too pretentious. How about Fiori; just Flowers?"

"Well . . ." he sat down close to her, leaving the end cushion free. "It is self-explanatory anyway."

Willow sipped her champagne. "Will I be expected to do all the flowers in the hotel?"

"Of course."

"Then I will need several assistants."

"Naturally."

She put her glass down on the table. "I will have an enormous amount to learn about growers, markets, distribution and so on before the hotel opens," she mused.

"I agree." He picked up her glass and handed it to her again. "Drink up. We must get through the bottle before we leave."

Stretching his arm along the back of the hammock he let it rest lightly across her shoulders. "I will send an experienced woman from Milan to help you for the first few months."

"Will she be my boss?"

He shook his head. "No. She will be your assistant. I will be financing the venture so I will be the boss."

She gave an inward sigh of relief. That hurdle was over anyway. "It is very generous of you."

The Italian shrugged his powerful shoulders. "I like to help young people. Business is business of course. One must see a good return on one's money. But you know that." He raised his glass. "Now let's drink a toast to the success and longevity of Fiori."

"Fiori!" cried Willow, enthusiastically draining her glass.

Picking up the bottle he refilled both glasses. "Another toast. To the success of the Paradiso without which Fiori could not start to bloom."

"The Paradiso!" She downed the entire drink, reached out to put down the glass, missed the edge of the table and to her horror heard the crystal shatter on the mosaic tiled floor.

She jumped up blushing furiously at her clumsiness. "I am so sorry!"

"Sit down," Bruno ordered calmly. "It is nothing. There are dozens more glasses."

He went inside the penthouse and Willow lay back on the cushions. She felt distinctly lightheaded. Champagne before dinner, three different wines during the meal and an hour or so later more champagne. Her eyelids felt unbearably heavy but it would never do to fall asleep during preliminary business discussions with her future employer. What she needed was something to eat. Staggering to her feet she helped herself to a peach and munched it, leaning on the balcony wall looking down at the three swimming pools.

It would be strange to live and work so near to Menton knowing that Pierre was just the other side of the border. Would he still visit the hotel after it had opened? Probably not, his involvement would have ended. Of course she would be able to visit old Anselm and might occasionally catch a glimpse of Pierre. Or Arlene. Or the baby.

She put the half-eaten peach down and, resting her elbows on the wall, lowered her face onto her folded arms. It was no good, all this absurd dreaming. If she accepted Bruno's offer she would have to put Pierre completely out of her mind. Somehow she would have to find the strength to cut him out of her life. It would be like amputating one of her limbs but it was the only way.

The sound of Bruno sweeping away broken glass made her turn. "Good," he said. "That's done. Now we will have a little music. It is a night for dancing."

Willow clung to the balcony for support. "Dancing? Oughtn't we go and inspect the shop?" Her tongue seemed too large for her mouth.

He walked back into the sitting room without replying and soon the sugar-sweet sound of popular music floated out to the patio.

Bruno stepped outside and held out his hand. "Come let us dance."

Willow looked round the tiny roof garden. "Here?"

He took her in his arms. "How much room do two people need?"

She hesitated. "Well I . . . I . . ."

"Relax," he murmured. "Relax and follow me. Look, I will show you. We move like this, and this, and this. Listen to the music. It is speaking to you. It is saying you have a fine, supple body. Use it. Indulge it. Dancing is a natural expression of pleasure. See how we compliment each other . . ."

Finally surrendering to the balmy night and the mellifluous persuasive voice, Willow allowed herself to respond to her partner's skill. Holding her close, his dry cheek pressed to hers, Bruno moved rhythmically around the patio, negotiating the space between the table and the hammock with easy grace. Soothed and lulled by the music, the moonlight and the sensuous movements of the Italian's fit body, she rested her heavy head on his shoulder. Her feet felt as if they were treading air. She was in Pierre's arms; they were dancing on the shining sea. Melodious waves of sound rose, fell, and sighed around them. They were no longer two people but one. One harmonious entity: one body, one mind, one spirit.

"*Bellissima, bellissima,*" her partner whispered.

She smiled. She felt as light as a feather. She could dance all night. On and on . . .

The music stopped. "You dance exquisitely," he breathed, gently blowing her hair away from her ear.

Still in a daze, she lifted her head, but it was Bruno holding her so close, not Pierre, and the hooded, hypnotic eyes gazing deeply into hers conveyed a message she understood all too well.

"*Carissima* . . ."

The full mouth fastened securely onto her lips and the strong hands held her in a vice-like grip, preventing her from making the least movement. Slowly he withdrew his lips, but his hands slipped down to her hips and the tantalizing curve of her buttocks.

"Beautiful, beautiful Willow, I am going to have you tonight," he murmured, straining her body even closer.

In a flash she realized that the whole evening, from the moment she had descended the stairs at Villa Martine, had been a gradual crescendo leading to this moment, and her champagne-fuddled mind was instantly clear about one thing. She had been a fool to think she could pit her wits against Bruno Ventura!

"Come." Keeping hold of her hand he pulled her towards the hammock.

Her feet slithered across the slippery tiles. "Just a minute!"

He stopped. "Yes?"

"I need a drink of water."

Snatching back her hand she walked rapidly indoors, through the dark sitting room and the bedroom into the bathroom and promptly locked the door.

Dizzy with relief she sank onto a chair and tried to take stock of her position.

It was beginning to look doubtful if she could

ever involve herself in business with Bruno Ventura. He was trying to make her drunk in order to make love to her. She must somehow outwit him. It was a long walk back to Menton!

The main problem was how to extricate herself from a situation rapidly becoming too hot to handle without an undignified scrimmage—or worse. If she faked illness he would be sure to see through it. If she pleaded her innocence it would simply excite his desire. If she struggled he would overpower her as easily as a lion brings down and ravages a gazelle.

Standing up she walked over to the wash basin, filled a glass with water and drank it in one draft. Her face, in the mirror, looked deathly pale and there were dark shadows under her anxious eyes. "Will you never learn?" she asked herself severely.

The minutes ticked by. If she stayed in the bathroom any longer he would come and look for her. He might even now be lying in wait in the bedroom ready to tackle her when she emerged. She splashed her face with cold water in an attempt to clear her head. Calm, calm she told herself, there's no need to be dramatic. If—as seemed most likely—he was still on the roof garden, she could slip through the sitting room into the anteroom and take the lift down before he noticed she had gone. Even if he came after her immediately he would hardly attack her in the presence of the security guard. Hopefully he would realize that he was beaten. She would then be able to persuade him to drive her back to

Menton. It was a far from perfect plan but it was the only one that came to mind immediately.

Quietly she unlocked the bathroom door and walked through the bedroom to the sitting room. Bruno was still outside, swinging gently to and fro on the hammock, smoking a fresh cigar.

Hardly daring to breathe she crept across the thick carpet taking care to avoid knocking against the furniture. Reaching the double doors she grasped the metal handle and pushed firmly down. Nothing happened. She tried again and again the door refused to budge.

"It's locked, my dear."

"Locked?" She spun 'round. The man on the patio had not moved. He was not even looking her way but gazing out to sea, his cigar glowing against the midnight-blue sky.

"Yes locked," he repeated. "You might as well come and sit down."

Willow stayed by the door. "But I would like to go back now." She forced a little laugh. "Or at least I would like to see the shop. After all it was our reason for coming."

"You are always in such a hurry," he said. "We have all night to look at the shop. I will get you back to Villa Martine safely I promise."

"But I want to go now," she insisted.

The Italian stood up, stretched in a leisurely manner and, strolling into the sitting room, switched on a table lamp. The sudden flood of light made Willow blink and turn her head away.

"You look like a mesmerized kitten," he said, smiling.

And you, she thought, look like a wily old wolf.

With every appearance of tranquillity she sat down in the nearest chair neatly laying her velvet jacket across her lap. "Why have you locked the door?"

"We don't want that fool Claudio walking in, do we?"

"Why not? Would it matter so much? I thought we were here to discuss business."

"My dear girl, it's far too early in the morning to discuss business." He began to saunter idly around the room, straightening a picture here, a magazine there, talking as he moved. "I brought you to the Paradiso so that you could gauge whether or not you would like to work here. The business details can be discussed at a later date."

"Bruno." Willow stroked the velvet jacket thoughtfully as if it were a sleeping cat. "What are the strings attached to this job?"

"Strings?" He sounded faintly puzzled.

"Yes."

Moving to the table behind the chair he extinguished his cigar. "Oh, now I understand." His voice dropped reproachfully. "You think I am blackmailing you to make love with me."

Without turning her head she knew he had moved behind her chair.

". . . I would never do such a thing," he continued softly, "even if I may hope that one day soon you will want me as much as I want you."

She sat very still, a muscle in her cheek beginning to twitch nervously.

"*Dio!* You are the sexiest little thing I have seen for months!' he breathed, swiftly encircling her from behind with arms like steel girders. "Let me show you the meaning of real pleasure. You will never regret it." His lips nuzzled the tender flesh at the side of her neck; his questing hands strayed to her breasts. . . .

"No!" Violently knocking away his hands Willow leapt to her feet. "Take me back to Menton! Now!"

Dodging his outstretched arms she marched to the door and rattled the handle noisily. "Let me out!"

The hooded eyes regarded her coldly. "You are not showing much sense, my dear."

She spun 'round, her eyes flashing. "What exactly do you mean?" At all costs she must not appear alarmed.

"I mean that you are in rather a weak position."

"Kindly explain."

"Simple. You want to run your own shop and I can help you."

"Ah!" She leaned against the door and folded her arms. "So now we have it. And you said no blackmail!"

He took a step towards her. She could almost feel the adrenaline pouring through her veins, preparing her body for the primitive instincts of fight or flight. In the dim lamplight he looked an ominous, menacing figure, his fleshy, olive-skinned face beaded with perspiration, his expensive grey-and-white striped shirt clinging damply to his chest. She remembered noting the snake-like eyes when he first removed his glasses in the study. Now their hard, ruthless expression was unmistakable. Mere stony slits under bruised lids, they gazed at her without tenderness.

"I want you," he said quietly. "Now. Tonight. You have an exciting, provocative young body and I am going to possess it. Just once." He smiled unpleasantly. "Or maybe twice. After tonight I give you my word that I will never trouble you again but I will help you in every way to set up your own business. Indeed I may never even want you again. There are, you understand, many women in my life."

"Then why bother with me?"

For a split second his eyes widened with anticipation. "Because you are a virgin and if I don't have you I know another man who will. First come, first served, my dear."

He moved to grab her but, ducking under his arm, she fled to the other end of the room knocking over a small table as she ran. Chortling with pleasure he came after her, moving with an athlete's speed and agility. Wildly she cast around for escape. The roof garden was no good; the only way out there was to jump over the balcony to certain death. Her eye lighted on the open bedroom door. If she could make it inside and turn the key in the lock she would be safe for a short time. Sprinting 'round the furniture she made as if to run out onto the patio, allowed him to come within a meter, doubled back on her tracks, dashed into the bedroom, closed the door and, leaning against it, groped for the key. No key! The sweat was trickling down her back. She felt the door give and, knowing her weight was no match for his, darted 'round the far side of the huge bed.

The Italian shoved open the door, made straight for the bathroom, whipped the key out of the lock and pocketed it.

Willow stared incredulously at the large head with its mane of gray hair. What kind of abnormal brain was contained in that thick skull? Health, wealth, power and influence were his yet he intended to rape an obscure English girl for her virginity.

"Give in," he urged. "I don't want to have to get rough with you. We Neopolitans don't have very nice manners when we are thwarted."

"I believe you," she said contemptuously.

Slowly, easily, knees slightly bent and arms flexed, he came towards her; the lion stalking the gazelle.

Before he could spring she leapt onto the bed, grabbed up a pillow and swung it at him with all her might. It hit the side of his head with a soft thud and his bellow of delighted laughter ricocheted around the walls of the room. Suddenly he lunged at her ankles, bringing her crashing down on the bed. In seconds he was on top of her, attempting to strip her dress from her body. Sinking her teeth in his shoulder, she bit down hard, tasted blood, heard his agonized yell, felt his grip weaken and threw him aside with a fierce strength she had not known she possessed. Rolling off the bed she picked herself up off the floor, flew to the door, wrenched it open and hurled herself into the sitting room, straight into the waiting arms of Pierre Castille.

Chapter Ten

"Well, well well!" he said, holding her at arm's length. "I hope you have had an amusing evening my dear? Yes, I can see you have. I am so glad. The party must have been a hell of a bore for a non-backgammon player."

Willow could hardly believe her ears. He was neither blind nor stupid; he must be aware of the situation!

He piloted her towards the terrace, stopping halfway across the room to pick up the table she had knocked over in her flight.

"I'm afraid I rather lost track of you, so I naturally assumed you'd had enough and gone to bed. As a matter of fact," he continued cheerfully, "it is pure chance I'm here. After everyone left I felt far too stimulated to sleep so I decided to return to the Paradiso and work. Coming up the drive I saw a light on in the penthouse and thinking it couldn't be Bruno because he was planning to return to Milan I decided I had better come in and switch it off."

"But the door was locked!" It was the first sentence she had managed to complete since his arrival.

"Of course. It is kept locked for security reasons. I used a master key."

A discreet cough from the bedroom doorway made them turn. An impeccably groomed Bruno —dark jacket over his shirt sleeves, tie securely knotted, hair neatly combed—sauntered towards them, cigar in hand. "I'm afraid I must apologise for abducting your lovely guest, Pierre. She expressed an interest in the Paradiso and I offered to give her a guided tour. She found it all so interesting that we stayed rather longer than we intended." He spread his hands in the apologetic gesture she had seen him use before. "I ought to have told you where we were going but you were showing signs of winning and I didn't want to disturb your concentration."

He had, she noticed, put on his tinted spectacles again.

Pierre laughed. "You were quite right. I did win. It was an excellent game. Victorine is a superb tactician. Matter of fact you did me a great favor. Although it meant neglecting her I couldn't allow my guest to be fleeced by that crowd of thugs. I am sure you agree."

Bruno nodded sagely. "Of course." Turning to Willow he inclined his head courteously. "Anyway it was my pleasure."

"He is a championship player, you know," Pierre said.

"Really?" Willow managed to feign an admiring expression.

The champion wandered nonchalantly out to the roof garden. "It is nothing," he said over his shoulder.

Pierre laughed. "You are an old hypocrite, Bruno."

The Italian grinned. "I'm afraid you are right my friend, but then you and I know each other well, do we not?" He reached for the champagne bottle. "I see there is still some left. Before you leave let us drink to the future of the Paradiso."

Pierre looked at his watch. "We ought to be going. I expect you want to catch an early flight and I must see that Willow gets her beauty sleep before facing my father in the morning. Did you bring a coat?" He made a move towards the bedroom. "I'll get it," she cried, sprinting ahead of him.

Once inside the room she closed the door and looked around for her jacket. It was lying innocently on the immaculate bedspread. Immaculate, that is, except for a tiny stain in the center. She really had drawn blood. Good! It looked like it would be the only retribution he would suffer!

The men were already waiting by the lift when she emerged. Down on the ground floor Bruno said good night to the security guard, patted Pepe affectionately on the rump and accompanied Pierre and Willow outside to the parked Ferrari.

"You'll let me know when you are coming

again?" Pierre said. "We must discuss that venti-
lation problem. I have some more drawings."

Bruno nodded. "Sometime next week."

"Good." Pierre opened the car door and Bruno
stepped forward and kissed her cheek.

"Good night exquisite Willow. It has been a
memorable evening for an old man." The tinted
spectacles glinted blankly in the yellow light
beaming out from the hotel, then he turned and
strolled back into the foyer puffing contentedly at
his cigar.

"Get in!" Pierre ordered in a harsh voice.

Quickly she slid into the Ferrari and he
slammed the door. Once in the driving seat he
switched on the engine with a flick of the wrist
and the car roared away from the hotel, climbed
the long drive at a furious speed, turned into the
road and raced towards the border. But this time
she was not in the least frightened, not frightened, that is, of Pierre's driving which, unlike
Bruno's, was perfectly controlled and inspired
absolute confidence. She was deeply alarmed
however by the expression on his face: the thin,
hard mouth; the taut skin stretched over the
clenched jaw; the familiar vein throbbing in his
temple. He was not merely angry; he was en-
raged.

Neither of them spoke a word during the drive.
Willow gazed out of the window nervously clasp-
ing and unclasping her hands in her lap, shooting
an occasional glance at the rock-like countenance
at her side.

Once they were through the border he slowed

the car down and when they reached the outskirts of the town he pulled up by the sea front and killed the engine. Still staring ahead he leaned back in his seat and folded his arms.

"Perhaps you had better explain yourself. I'm sure you are itching to get it off your chest."

Treat a mad dog with caution! "What exactly do you want me to explain?" she inquired mildly.

"Oh come on!" he mocked. "You're not as innocent as all that. You walk out on my party late at night with the randiest man in the room and hours later I find you in the locked penthouse half-dressed, wild-eyed, over-excited—and you expect me to believe . . ." Swinging 'round he seized her by the shoulders and shook her until her teeth rattled.

For an instant a red haze of rage welled up in front of her eyes then, raising her arm she struck him a mighty blow across the side of the head knocking him back against the window. "Take your obscene mind home to bed—I need some air!" Throwing open the car door she ran across the pavement and tore off her high-heeled sandals, throwing them onto the beach.

Heedless of the sharp stones cutting into her bare feet she dashed across the beach and plumped herself down in front of the water. After a while the sound of the silvery waves lapping tranquilly against the shingle and the gentle breeze fanning her hot face began to calm her. She had acted in an infantile manner. There was no possible excuse for her rudeness and her stupidity. Of course Pierre was angry! Turning she saw him sitting on a rock in the moonlight dangling her sandals from one hand. Standing up she walked slowly back towards him.

"I'm sorry," she said simply.

He tossed over her shoes. "The party's over, Cinderella. Time to climb aboard the pumpkin."

She looked down at the shredded dress clinging to her legs. "I've certainly ruined the ball gown!"

He smiled wryly. "I think that's the least of our problems." Wearily he rubbed his forehead. "Look, today has lasted a very long time. May we go?"

"No." She sat firmly down on a rock. "Not until I have told you everything."

He shook his head. "I am no longer interested. I just want to take my dirty mind home to my nice clean bed."

"Then you'd better go," she said, "because unless you give me a hearing I am staying right here."

"I see." He gave a resigned sigh. "All right, but make it brief, will you?"

Willow bit her lip. She must find the right words to make him understand. Even if his own behavior had been inexcusable she could not allow him to think the same of her. To return to England knowing that he despised her as a mere tart would be unbearable.

"Well go on." Pierre's face assumed an expression of unutterable boredom.

"I went with Bruno," she began calmly, "because he offered me premises for a flower shop in the Paradiso. He said I ought to look at them tonight as he had to go to Milan in the morning."

The bored expression changed to one of incredulity. "He did what?"

"I am a competent florist and I speak Italian," she said defensively. "It seemed a reasonable suggestion."

He leaned forward. "Exactly where was this shop to be sited?"

She frowned. "In the shopping complex of course."

Pierre's tense body shook with silent, grim laughter. "But there is no shopping complex. There will be a hairdressing business, that's all. Shops were never even considered. Anyway why would the guests need to buy flowers? The hotel will naturally contract out its business to a local firm."

Willow dug a hole in the shingle with the heel of her sandal. "I see."

"I knew you would be in trouble with Ventura," Pierre said. "That's why I came after you."

"I see." The stupid hole kept refilling; doggedly, she kept digging it out again.

"Stop playing with those stones and tell me the rest!"

Dropping the sandal she wrapped her arms around her legs and rested her chin on her knees. "You won't like it."

"Never mind. Go on."

"Well to start with he played a tape of Neopolitan songs which made him cry. . . ."

Pierre uttered a mirthless laugh.

"Then he drove like a mad thing all the way to the hotel almost as though he wanted to soften me up, to frighten me before we got there."

Pierre groaned. "*Mon Dieu!* And I did the same thing to you coming back!"

"No. Your driving was quite different—fast but controlled. He drove insanely. I really thought we would have an accident. Anyway we arrived safely and he showed me 'round the hotel."

"Didn't you ask to see the shop?"

"Of course. But he kept putting me off, saying we had plenty of time and so on. Afterwards he insisted on going up to the penthouse and opening a bottle of champagne."

"And then?"

Willow shivered. "I'm getting cold."

"What happened then?" he insisted.

"What do you mean?"

Pierre dropped his head into his hands. "Ye gods grant me patience! What happened after the champagne?"

"We danced," she said reluctantly.

He lifted his head. "Oh yes? How?"

"How do you think? Standing up facing each other and moving our feet in time to the music."

"Your feet and everything else. I suppose his arms were around you?"

"Of course."

"And yours were 'round his neck?"

"Some of the time, yes."

"And your head on his shoulder?"

"I . . . I can't remember."

"And he held you close—"

"Stop it! Stop it!" Picking up a handful of pebbles she hurled them at his legs.

In a flash he was crouching before her, gripping her wrists with both hands, his eyes blazing with fury. "You enjoyed it didn't you? Confess it. You really enjoyed being fondled by that depraved old *roué*."

"All right," she admitted between gritted teeth. "I did enjoy it. I adored it. It was like dancing on air, dancing in heaven. I could have gone on and on and on because . . ."

"Yes?"

"Because I imagined I was dancing with . . ."

The grip on her wrists tightened. "Yes?"

"With someone else," she finished lamely.

"I see." He flung her away in disgust. "That raw youth staying at the Grande I suppose. You'd better tell me what happened after that."

"He tried to rape me," she said dully.

"And did he succeed?"

Sitting up, she began to strap on a sandal.

"Answer the question!" Pierre shouted.

Lifting her head she looked at him with empty, hopeless eyes. "No. And you can believe that or not—I don't really care."

The sound of a wave shushing against the stones was followed by Pierre's long sigh of relief. Willow put on the other sandal. She felt cold and shivery. "May we go back now?"

Pierre stood up and pulled her to her feet. Taking off his jacket he draped it 'round her shoulders.

The unexpectedly tender gesture suddenly melted the knotted lump of shame and resentment in her chest and flinging herself at him she clung to him as tightly as if she were drowning in a sea of sorrows. "I'm sorry," she sobbed.

Gently he raised her head and tried to stroke

away her tears with his fingers. "I know. I know. I know."

Still sobbing she reached up, pulled his head down and pressed her wet lips to his mouth. He responded like a man parched with thirst, drinking in her salt tears and holding her close to his trembling body, then, with a deep groan, he thrust her roughly aside and strode off up the beach leaving her to stumble miserably after him—a small, bedraggled figure, weeping bitterly.

The journey through the dormant town was quick and silent except for Willow's sobs. When they became more than he could bear Pierre dug into his trouser pocket and passed her a clean folded handkerchief. Taking the hint, she dried her eyes, blew her nose and endeavored to control the jarring spasms which made her gasp for air.

Villa Martine's terrace lights were still on but otherwise the house was dark. Taking her arm he led her up the steps. In the hall he took back his jacket and replaced it with hers.

"Go up to bed," he said. "In the morning we must talk but now we must both get some sleep." And crossing the hall he went into the study and closed the door.

Willow dragged herself up the wide, shallow stairs to her room. Sleep! However exhausted, she would never be able to sleep. How could she sleep when her mind kept going over and over the events of the past few hours? She took off Inigo's costly, ruined creation and dropped it on the floor, stood under the hot shower, wrapped herself in a huge bath towel and sat down in an armchair to think.

It was over. Finished. Not that anything had actually begun—a few kisses, however honeyed, hardly constituted a serious love affair. Pierre would never forgive her the night's folly. Unable to contain herself, she had rashly tried to express her love and gratitude in that passionate kiss and he had rejected violently. He plainly thought she had given herself to Bruno Ventura hoping he would back her business and he could reasonably argue that if she were capable of such a thing once, then she had most likely done it before and would do it again when the occasion warranted.

It was impossible to continue living in his house knowing how much he despised her. Anyway Arlene would soon return from Paris and the sight of them together day in and day out would surely break her heart. It was time for her to leave.

Getting up, she pulled on a skirt and sweater, lugged her suitcase out of the cupboard, tossed in all her belongings and fastened the locks. She then sat down at the dressing table and wrote a few lines on the thick engraved paper Pierre provided for his guests.

"Dear Anselm, I hate myself for running out on you but I have to do it. I will never forget you. Willow."

If she popped it on the easel he would find it in the morning. Poor Anselm. He would be so disappointed, especially as he would never know what had occurred in the middle of the night to make her leave so hurriedly.

Picking up the case she opened the door and

went out onto the landing. Pierre's door was closed, so was Anselm's. Leaving the suitcase at the head of the main staircase she walked quietly up to the second floor and made her way down the dark passage to the studio.

To her surprise the closed door emitted a thin strip of light. She hesitated. He must have gone to bed without extinguishing the light. Quietly she turned the handle and went in.

The old man was sitting in the high-backed cane chair dressed in an old red robe and felt slippers, reading a book. The angle-poise light at his side beamed down on his patriarchal head as on a figure in an early Italian masterpiece.

It was too late to withdraw. He looked up and smiled. "This is the pleasantest thing that has happened to me in many a long wakeful night. Come in my dear."

"I'm going away," she blurted. "I was going to leave this for you." She waved the note in the air.

He put down his book. "Why?"

She shook her head. "It's too complicated to explain. I'm sorry. I really am sorry, Anselm. I know it will ruin the portrait and you are counting on it for the exhibition. It's a rotten way to treat you after all your kindness. I feel awful."

"Hush. You are upsetting yourself unnecessarily." Getting up he came over and led her back to the chair he had just vacated. "Sit down for a moment. I promise not to try to change your mind. You obviously have your own good reasons. But where are you going?"

"To the airport."

He glanced at the clock. "You'll have rather a

long wait. I don't suppose you'll get a plane until the morning."

"I don't care," she said stubbornly.

The old man nodded. "That's all right then. Before you go, my dear, would you do something for me?"

"If I can."

"It's nothing too onerous. Just stay where you are for a few minutes while I make some minor adjustments to the portrait. It won't be as satisfactory as if you completed the sittings but it won't be entirely a lost cause."

She looked out of the window. The moon had slipped out of sight. "I must leave before it gets light."

"Of course," he agreed. "Now let's see what we can do to save the picture." Switching on the strip lighting he settled onto his high stool and began to select his brushes. "I'm sorry you never met my wife," he said suddenly. "She would have loved you. She had a very individual beauty when young—not to everyone's taste but very endearing to me. More important she had a kind heart and a loving forgiving spirit."

"You must miss her."

"I do, I do." Leaning back on the stool he squinted at the canvas and, leaning forward again, began to paint. "She died many years ago but I still miss her every day of my life and do you know I believe Pierre does too."

"Really?" At the mention of his name Willow automatically clutched at the material of her skirt.

The painter's pale, observant eyes registered the convulsive movement. "Yes. He is very like his mother in many ways although he is inclined to sum up people and situations too quickly and regret it afterwards."

Willow remained silent. She had never witnessed Pierre's regret!

"Of course," Anselm continued, "he has never been the same person since Natalie's death."

"His mother?"

"No, no, not his mother. His fiancée."

"His fiancée? When did she die?"

Anselm gazed thoughtfully at the rounded curve of his subject's cheek. "Oh, it must be eight years ago now . . ."

"What happened?"

He sighed heavily. "It was a terrible time for all of us. Natalie was married to Pierre's good friend, Paul Vincent. Pierre and Paul were at school together and, owing to family circumstances, Paul spent most of his childhood with us. He joined the diplomatic service and eventually took his little family—Natalie and their small son Marcel—to Turkey for a tour of duty. They were so excited about going. Even now I recall Natalie's radiant little face. When they arrived they were completely captivated by the place, the people, everything. They built their own house and five-year-old Marcel soon spoke the language as fluently as his own. Paul even began to talk about giving up his diplomatic career and going into business there. They really seemed to have found their own piece of heaven on earth." He paused.

Willow leaned forward. "Yes?"

Anselm rested his brush across his palette. "I find it difficult to talk about. You see we knew them so well—they were part of the family. Anyway . . ." He put down the palette and wiped his hands on a rag. "To cut a painful story short, there was an earth tremor, nothing spectacular, very few people were hurt but the Vincent's house and those nearby suffered extensive damage. Paul was killed and Natalie and the boy sufficiently injured to be detained in hospital for several weeks. The house caught fire. Everything was lost. Everything."

Willow's expressive eyes filled with compassion. "How dreadful."

Anselm, visibly agitated, got off the stool and began to pace around the room. "I'm afraid there is worse to come. As soon as they were released from hospital Pierre flew out and brought them back here. The poor girl was in a terrible state. She had lost her husband, her home, the lot. She was thin and nervous—nothing like the cheerful Natalie we remembered. Pierre was so good and patient with her and, over the months, I believe they grew really fond of one another. She depended on him for everything and the boy adored him. Eventually they decided to get married. I personally believe—though we never discussed it—that Pierre felt he owed it to his dead friend to see that his wife and son reached a safe harbor."

He stopped talking and, unscrewing the lid of a bottle of white spirit, poured some into a jar.

Willow waited. It was no use saying Yes? or What happened next? He was obviously deeply moved by the story and would finish it in his own time.

"The portrait will be fine," he said irrelevantly. "I hope you will see it one day."

"I hope so too."

He screwed the cap on the bottle and put it back on the shelf. "Natalie and Marcel were killed one afternoon in a multiple car accident. Pierre had gone to meet them off a Paris flight. She had been helping a friend move into an apartment and was exhausted—nevertheless, she insisted on driving." He sighed. "I'm afraid she was largely to blame—trying to overtake, you know how it is. Pierre was thrown clear but in spite of a broken arm and a fearful gash across his face—you must have noticed the scar—he dove back into the wreckage to try and get them out. It was hopeless . . ."

The old man leaned wearily against the table. To Willow he seemed to have suddenly shrunk inside his red robe.

". . . they were both dead." His voice quavered. "He did everything he could, my son. Once he knew it was useless he plunged into the other cars—some of them blazing fiercely—and dragged out anyone he could lay his hands on. Three people, including a baby girl, owed their lives to Pierre. Six died." He passed his hand unhappily across his eyebrows. "I haven't talked about it for years. Years. Amazing how these things go on upsetting one." He smiled briefly. "I can't think why I am boring you with the whole thing."

Willow swallowed in sympathy. "It must have been terrible for you all. Pierre's face . . . ?"

Anselm straightened his bowed back and returned to his stool. "He was an awful mess but the doctors soon patched him up. He refused to have plastic surgery though. Said he wanted to remember—whatever that meant."

"I think I know," she said softly. "Do you think he blamed himself?"

Anselm nodded. "I know he did. He said so time and time again. "I ought to have been driving," he kept saying. But if the truth be told, Natalie was a headstrong girl. She liked to have her own way and after all she had been through such a harrowing time. He has never recovered you know. There is a scar inside him as well as on his face. He used to laugh all the time."

"Has he never . . . wanted to marry anyone else?"

Anselm shrugged. "I have no idea. There have been other women of course, some of them charming and intelligent. But whether he thinks it would be a kind of betrayal or whether—I simply don't know. . . ." His voice faded away and he sat slumped on the stool looking very tired and very old.

Impulsively Willow stood up, walked across and put her arms around the thin, brittle shoulders. "Thank you for telling me."

"But you are still leaving?"

She steeled herself against the appeal in his voice. "Yes. I'm afraid I must still go. And you, my friend, must go to bed. What are you doing up at this time of night anyway?"

"You will understand," he said smiling, "when you are eighty-four." Standing up he kissed her on both cheeks. "*Au revoir*, enchanting Willow. I hope we meet again before I have to make that last lonely journey."

She threw her arms around the frail figure. "Don't talk like that! Of course we will meet again. Of course!"

"If you are so sure then there's no need to cry is there?" he said gently loosening the embrace. "Now we must be practical. How do you intend to get to the airport?"

"I shall walk into Menton and get a taxi."

"Carrying a heavy suitcase I suppose?"

"Well, yes."

"Come, come, my child don't be so foolish. Let me telephone the taxi."

"All right. But it must wait outside the gates. I don't want—"

"I know, I know." He patted her arm understandingly.

They looked at one another: the famous old artist already serenely anticipating his own death and the girl whose vibrant youth had imbued his painting with renewed purpose and vigour.

"Don't be afraid to love," he said. "It is the only thing—absolutely the only thing—that makes life worth living."

Willow nodded silently and walked quickly to the door. Without looking 'round she said abruptly, "If he asks, just say thanks, will you?"

"I will," the quiet voice assured her.

She walked rapidly along the passage and down the stairs. Crossing the landing she picked up the suitcase and continued down the main staircase through the hall to the vestibule followed all the way by the heavy heartbreaking scent of flowers. Unbolting the front door she stepped out onto the terrace. Good-bye Villa Martine. Good-bye. Going down the steps she touched the pale, conical wisteria blooms as she passed. Good-bye, good-bye. Trudging down the long drive she gave the dreaming roses a last long look. Good-bye, sleep well.

Reaching the great wrought iron gates she put down the suitcase and turning looked back at Pierre's darkened window. Good-bye my love. My love. My love.

A car drew up beside her and the driver leaned out, exhaling a cloud of strong tobacco smoke. "You the lady wanting a taxi?"

"Yes." She opened the door and pushed her case inside. "Will you take me up to Colombaia please."

The man spat noisily out of the window. "Colombaia! Don't you tourists ever need to sleep?"

Chapter Eleven

Willow's car was still standing in the square where she had left it almost a week earlier. It had been raining. The trees dripped steadily onto the stones with a gentle plopping sound. The chairs outside the *Bar et Tabac* were tipped against the tables as though reserved for a crowd of nocturnal VIPs.

In front of her the solid facade of the church loomed. Next to the Post Office was the *Épicerie* where she had first seen Anselm emerge burdened with groceries. That was the moment the whole thing had started. If she had not rushed forward to help him she would never have seen Pierre again. The bold disturbing kiss on the mountain road would have been no more than a curious episode, an amusing story to tell her friends at home. The holiday would have passed enjoyably but uneventfully and she would have returned to England almost the same person as when she left.

She opened the trunk of the car and shoved her case inside. The noise of the lid closing sounded sharp, metallic and horribly final in the night air. Suddenly she knew, with great certainty, what she must do. She must telephone Steven at the Grande and tell him that she had changed her mind; she would return to England with him and marry him whenever he wanted. After all, in a sense she owed it to him. For months she had led him to believe that she loved him and wanted to get married. The fact that she had fallen hopelessly in love with another man was not Steven's fault. He was still the same person she had thought she loved and he needed her. His mother was not a fit woman and his father was getting on in age. They needed her too—whether or not they realized it! If she gave up working she could take over a number of jobs on the farm.

And she was still fond of Steve. You couldn't suddenly stop being fond of someone because you discovered you loved someone else. Anyway life away from Pierre would be no life. Her real life had, in essence, begun and ended within the space of a few weeks. What happened now was of no importance.

It would be no sacrifice to marry Steven, it was the logical, sensible and right thing to do. Her business ambitions would go down the drain, but the marriage would at least mean that she could safeguard her father's future.

Feeling under the stone Willow pulled out the key to Number Nine and let herself inside. First she must clean the house, then she would gather the rest of her things and put them by the front door. After that she would snatch an hours sleep before going to the hotel to telephone Steven. On reflection it had been rather stupid to pull the telephone cord out of the wall in a fit of pique on her first day. She would have to pay to have it reconnected.

Methodically she swept through the kitchen, larder and hall and washed the coffee cups still in the sink. Moving on she swept the spiral stairs; vacuumed the first landing, bedroom and bathroom; cleaned the bath and put out fresh towels; dusted the bedroom; put on clean sheets and carried the bundle of laundry down to the hall for Anna Leduc to take to the local laundress.

It seemed a lot of work for the short time she had spent in the house and by the time it was finished she was extremely tired and still had not touched the top stairs and the sitting room.

She undressed, slipped on a bathrobe, closed the door and the shutters and lay down on the bed, taking care not to rumple the sheets. The sitting room could wait.

But sleep would not come. Weary though she was her alert mind denied her body the peace and rest it craved. Over and over she debated the same question: Should she leave without seeing Pierre again, without thanking him for rescuing her from the mountain and taking her into his house? Should she at least telephone him? Or would it be better to write him a note when she reached home, a short formal note of thanks? He would probably read it, tear it in half and drop it in the wastepaper basket. Well let him! At least she would have discharged her obligations! She sighed restlessly.

It was useless to try to sleep any longer. She might as well finish cleaning the house.

Getting up, she padded down to the kitchen, collected a bag of cleaning materials, took it upstairs, and thrust it over the top step into the sitting room. Returning with the vacuum cleaner she dumped it on the floor and started to dust the books on the table at the back of the room.

Gradually she became aware of a strange feeling—a tingling in the scalp, a slight chill between the shoulder blades. Impatiently she shook her head and went on dusting, carefully picking up book after book. Her nerves must be in a more jangled state than she realized. But it came again—the distinct impression that she was being watched. Slowly, fearfully, she turned, gasped and dropped the duster and the book. Pierre was lying on the chaise on the balcony staring at her through the glass doors with the saddest eyes she had ever seen in the face of any man.

For perhaps two whole minutes they stared at each other without moving, Willow's heart clammering to be loosed from her chest. Still staring as though hypnotized, she dropped to her haunches and picked up the book. It was a large atlas and she pressed it to her bosom hoping to quiet the pounding of her heart.

When they moved they moved simultaneously.

Pierre stood up and Willow, her legs shaking as though she had just run a mile, crossed to the French doors.

"Let me in." His voice sounded muffled through the glass. He looked terrible—haggard and exhausted. Suddenly frantic, Willow unlocked the doors and wrenched them apart. Slipping to the floor she buried her head in her hands and all of the heartache of the night poured from her in a torrent of anguished sobs.

When she finally lifted her pale, tear-drowned face he was gazing at her from the open doors.

"Why do I always make you cry?" he said, more to himself than to her. "You breeze into my life upsetting all my plans. You allow me to think . . . to believe that heaven is within . . . that we had finally reached some kind of . . . Then you take off in the middle of the night with a smooth operator like Ventura—a man incidentally with whom I never intend to do business again—and when I finally manage to get you home without involving you in a punch-up you walk out for good, telling my father you are going to the airport. No explanation. No good-bye. Nothing. If you don't call that being cruel and unfeeling may I ask how you would define those words?"

Willow swallowed hard, wiped her eyes with her sleeve and drew a deep shuddering breath. "Let me reverse the question. Would you call a man cruel who tried—more than once—to seduce a girl, unsophisticated and probably rather impressionable, while he was still living with his pregnant mistress?"

"I would," he agreed. "I would call him very cruel. Despicable in fact."

"Oh."

"You sound surprised."

"I didn't realize you would condemn yourself so readily." She dabbed ineffectually at her wet cheeks with the damp robe.

"So, you are running away from the licentious Frenchman into the arms of the stolid, loyal English lad I met yesterday. Right?"

"Right."

"Allow me to congratulate you."

She looked up, her swimming eyes appealing for clemency and, drawing a deep breath, she made a final desperate bid for his understanding. "I have never used drugs, slept around or done any of the things that some people now regard as normal behavior. I am not congratulating myself or anything. Far from it. I am no better or worse than average. If I had wanted to make love to anyone who bought me a coffee, I would have done so. My problem is—has always been—that I'm just not like that."

He gave her a brief sad smile. "You don't have to tell me, I know. I have always known."

"Then why did you try to . . ."

He pointed an admonishing finger. "You have been listening at doors again. You know what happens to people who do that."

A faint blush stole up her creamy throat to her pale cheeks. "They hear no good of themselves."

"More than that—they only get half the story. I assume you overheard Arlene telling me she was pregnant and you concluded that we were lovers?"

Willow nodded silently. "As a matter of fact," Pierre said lightly, "I will make a very good uncle."

"An uncle?" Her jaw dropped.

"Yes. Arlene is my sister-in-law. My brother Ludo is in Saudi Arabia on an engineering project. Arlene's pregnancy is the result of his last visit. She cannot go out there until he finds suitable accommodations and now she is pregnant it is doubtful that the heat would agree with her. My father and I will take care of her until Ludo returns. Three months at the most. I am building a house for them just outside Paris. She is thrilled with it."

Willow dropped her flaming face into her hands. Dear Lord. She had made such a fool of herself!

"Why didn't you ask me about Arlene?" he asked gently.

She kept her face averted. How could she ever look into his eyes again? "It all seemed so private, so personal. Anyway your life was so different from mine and I thought you had different values too. Of course I should never have assumed. It was stupid. Perhaps if my mother had lived she would have helped me to—I don't know— mature?"

The Frenchman gazed compassionately at the little figure crouched on the floor. "Ah yes. Perhaps." He stretched his long limbs luxuriously.

Willow, peeping over her bent knees, watched him walk outside and take in great lungfuls of morning air.

The sun, playing about his head, lit up the gray threads in the dark hair and she experienced a wild longing to rush over and put her arms around him, to kiss away the tired, vulnerable expression she had never seen before. But remembering that she had done so once that night already, and had been severely repulsed, nothing on earth would induce her to do it again. Besides which, now that he knew her for the foolish ignorant person she really was, any interest he might have felt must surely have been extinguished. At this moment he was probably thanking his lucky stars he had not become more deeply involved.

Pierre looked over his shoulder. "Come here."

She got up and joined him.

"Look out there," he said, indicating the green valley swooping down to the glittering sea. "I have enjoyed that view all my life. This progressive age has done its best to destroy all that but failed thank God!"

"All your life? But . . ."

He nodded. "I grew up in this house. Nine Rue des Fleurs was our home. Ludo and I slept upstairs and my mother and father had this room. We were quite poor. My father's great success came to him comparatively late in life. When Ludo and I grew up he bought a smaller house and I took over this one. I use it as a hideaway. I believe I am happier here than anywhere."

"So I am renting it from you?"

"Yes. Do you mind?"

"N-no, I don't think so. It's a bit of a surprise that's all." Together they watched the first bus of the day grinding its way up the steep hill below.

"I never wanted to love anyone as much as I love you," Pierre said suddenly.

Willow's heart stopped. For a fraction of time it ceased to beat then began to pound crazily against the wall of her chest, filling her ears with its jubilant din.

"After Natalie and the boy died," Pierre said, "I swore I would never be responsible for another human being, and, apart from my father, I never have. You see if I had been driving that afternoon . . ." His voice cracked.

Willow placed her hand lightly over his. "Did you love her very much?"

He shook his head. "In retrospect, no. I was fond of her of course and we got along well together but I felt I owed it to Paul—who was closer to me than my own brother—to see that his wife and son were cared for. In the end I destroyed them."

Willow tightened her grip on his arm. "But it was not your fault. It's no good blaming yourself for something you could never have prevented. Maybe if you had been driving it might not have happened, but she wanted to drive—Anselm told me all about it. He said she was headstrong, nervous, totally shattered by the earthquake and her husband's death. If you had insisted on driving what would her reaction have been?"

He shrugged. "I don't know."

"You do!"

"She would have become hysterical," he admitted slowly. "She was like that. Sweet one moment, a mad thing the next. She couldn't help it."

"Of course not, but it is wrong of you to go on ruining your life, tormenting yourself for something you did in good faith." For a brief, very brief moment they seemed to have changed roles —she to the consoler, he to the consoled.

"The photographs in your office," Willow said tentatively, "are they of Marcel?"

"Yes, he was a delightful child—" Pierre stopped abruptly, unable to bear the memory.

"I wish I had known him," she said softly.

He turned to face her. "I have never talked to anyone like this."

Seizing her hand he pulled her back into the room and, holding her at arm's length, stared hungrily at her tearstained face—frustration, pain and longing blazing in his eyes.

"I didn't want to love you in case I hurt you too. If anything happened to you because of me . . ."

"Or you because of me."

He frowned, puzzled. "What do you mean?"

"It's life, Pierre. We are all subject to its hazards. You might have killed yourself, climbing up the trellis on the balcony." She chided him gently.

His mouth quirked into a wicked grin. "Ludo and I used to climb up and down regularly when we were kids, but I came through the front door this time. I was up here for ages before you arrived."

"I made a resolution," Willow said.

He shook his head in mock reproof. "It's not the New Year. You had no business making resolutions."

"I know." Her green eyes glinted mischievously. "And the trouble is I may not be able to keep this one."

He laughed—one of his rare shouts of delight, and grabbing her 'round the waist whirled her 'round and 'round until she was dizzy, then propping her against the wall, he stood back, his face suddenly grave.

"I love you, Willow."

"I love you, Pierre."

His eyes—bluer than the Mediterranean, bluer than the sky above it, bluer than the gentians growing on the mountain—slowly darkened with desire.

"Once before I asked you trust me. Do you remember?"

"I do."

"Do you trust me now?"

She nodded, her whole face alight with the response he was waiting for.

"Take off your robe."

She did not hesitate. Undoing the sash she let the garment slip from her shoulders and stood before him naked.

He reached out and, taking her hand, raised her arm above her slowly, as if beginning a courtly dance, walked 'round her in a circle gazing at her with awe and wonder. "My God but you are lovely," he breathed, relinquishing her hand. "I am almost afraid to touch you."

She took a step towards him, her emerald eyes fixed on his enraptured face. "If you don't," she said quietly, "I think I might die."

Still advancing, Willow shook her head, her bright hair bobbing about her flushed face, her eyes glazed with love. "No. No more talking."

Pierre placed his hands on her shoulders, holding her off. "You must listen," he said gravely. "Before I completely lose control I want you to know that you are, at this moment, as irrevocably my precious, my beloved, my adoring wife, as you will be afterwards—or after any ceremony, civil or religious, that anyone may perform over us later. Do you believe me?"

"I believe you," she whispered.

Passion flared like a beacon between them. Willow closed her eyes and felt his arms go around her sweeping her into the air. Then she was lying on the floor, his naked limbs covering hers, his lips and hands at last permitted the freedom they longed for, exploring and teasing every sensitive inch of her sensually starved body. Her consciousness ebbed away and her mind, a cyclone of sound and image, gradually distanced itself from her thrilled, sweetly tormented flesh. Abandoning herself to her deepest instinct she reached out to pleasure his ardent manhood, joining him in the divine, protracted rhythm of love: the act of giving and receiving pure joy with which men and women, inheritors of this heaven and hell called Earth, have delighted and comforted each other since time immemorial.

Silhouette Romance

IT'S YOUR OWN SPECIAL TIME
Contemporary romances for today's women.
Each month, six very special love stories will be yours
from SILHOUETTE.

$1.75 each

☐ 100 Stanford	☐ 128 Hampson	☐ 157 Vitek	☐ 184 Hardy
☐ 101 Hardy	☐ 129 Converse	☐ 158 Reynolds	☐ 185 Hampson
☐ 102 Hastings	☐ 130 Hardy	☐ 159 Tracy	☐ 186 Howard
☐ 103 Cork	☐ 131 Stanford	☐ 160 Hampson	☐ 187 Scott
☐ 104 Vitek	☐ 132 Wisdom	☐ 161 Trent	☐ 188 Cork
☐ 105 Eden	☐ 133 Rowe	☐ 162 Ashby	☐ 189 Stephens
☐ 106 Dailey	☐ 134 Charles	☐ 163 Roberts	☐ 190 Hampson
☐ 107 Bright	☐ 135 Logan	☐ 164 Browning	☐ 191 Browning
☐ 108 Hampson	☐ 136 Hampson	☐ 165 Young	☐ 192 John
☐ 109 Vernon	☐ 137 Hunter	☐ 166 Wisdom	☐ 193 Trent
☐ 110 Trent	☐ 138 Wilson	☐ 167 Hunter	☐ 194 Barry
☐ 111 South	☐ 139 Vitek	☐ 168 Carr	☐ 195 Dailey
☐ 112 Stanford	☐ 140 Erskine	☐ 169 Scott	☐ 196 Hampson
☐ 113 Browning	☐ 142 Browning	☐ 170 Ripy	☐ 197 Summers
☐ 114 Michaels	☐ 143 Roberts	☐ 171 Hill	☐ 198 Hunter
☐ 115 John	☐ 144 Goforth	☐ 172 Browning	☐ 199 Roberts
☐ 116 Lindley	☐ 145 Hope	☐ 173 Camp	☐ 200 Lloyd
☐ 117 Scott	☐ 146 Michaels	☐ 174 Sinclair	☐ 201 Starr
☐ 118 Dailey	☐ 147 Hampson	☐ 175 Jarrett	☐ 202 Hampson
☐ 119 Hampson	☐ 148 Cork	☐ 176 Vitek	☐ 203 Browning
☐ 120 Carroll	☐ 149 Saunders	☐ 177 Dailey	☐ 204 Carroll
☐ 121 Langan	☐ 150 Major	☐ 178 Hampson	☐ 205 Maxam
☐ 122 Scofield	☐ 151 Hampson	☐ 179 Beckman	☐ 206 Manning
☐ 123 Sinclair	☐ 152 Halston	☐ 180 Roberts	☐ 207 Windham
☐ 124 Beckman	☐ 153 Dailey	☐ 181 Terrill	
☐ 125 Bright	☐ 154 Beckman	☐ 182 Clay	
☐ 126 St. George	☐ 155 Hampson	☐ 183 Stanley	
☐ 127 Roberts	☐ 156 Sawyer		

READERS' COMMENTS ON SILHOUETTE ROMANCES:

"I would like to congratulate you on the most wonderful books I've had the pleasure of reading. They are a tremendous joy to those of us who have yet to meet the man of our dreams. From reading your books I quite truly believe that he will some-day appear before me like a prince!"

—L.L.*, Hollandale, MS

"Your books are great, wholesome fiction, always with an upbeat, happy ending. Thank you."

—M.D., Massena, NY

"My boyfriend always teases me about Silhouette Books. He asks me, how's my love life and natu-rally I say terrific, but I tell him that there is always room for a little more romance from Sil-houette."

—F.N., Ontario, Canada

"I would like to sincerely express my gratitude to you and your staff for bringing the pleasure of your publications to my attention. Your books are well written, mature and very contemporary."

—D.D., Staten Island, NY

*names available on request